TIDAL WAVE

FLORIDA COAST ADVENTURES BOOK 2

JOHNNY ASA

<u>Sign up to my newsletter here.</u> If you do, I'll let you know when the next book comes out.

Visit me on Facebook or on the web at JohnnyAsa.com for all the latest updates.

1

I paused, water bottle halfway to my lips and tried to remember how I'd wound up on a fishing boat. After I'd come up to Florida to rescue my dad from a gang of drug dealers, I'd wanted to head back home, but it didn't take long for the idea of leaving my dad and Mary Ann just to go back to being a long-distance truck driver to rub me the wrong way.

"Billy, is everything okay?" my dad said as he gestured at me from behind the wheel. He was wearing a life jacket, a white captain's hat, and a pair of board shorts so bright, they hurt to look at.

"Yeah, everything is fine, Dad," I said, waving at him with one hand as a gust of wind hit me in the face, blowing my fishing hat off my head. The strap around my neck caught the hat, keeping it from going overboard as I grabbed it and put it back on my head. "Just grabbing a quick drink." I wiped my head with the back of one hand and flung the sweat away. "Still not used to the heat out here."

"It's fine. You just looked a bit lost." He shook his head for a second. "Look, I know the job isn't what you had in mind, but it's honest work." He smiled at me. "'Sides, I really enjoy spending the time with you. I won't be around forever, after all."

"I like spending time with you too, Dad. You know that. And the job's great," I said, glancing around the charter boat we ran together. "What I really love is working with tourists and helping them try to catch sailfish." I shrugged because it was mostly true. Helping dad out on the boat while he drove around tourists definitely beat trucking across the good old US of A and sleeping in the dingy back cabin of my truck.

It even paid pretty well since dad gave me thirty percent of the take after expenses, and I got to stay at his place rent free. At a couple hundred bucks per person, the take could be sizeable since we generally had groups of six to twelve.

That had been six months ago, and I was starting to worry I'd settled, that after everything I'd done to try to escape this small Florida coast town, Pleasantville had pulled me back in like a magnet.

"Then why do you seem like you've got one foot out the door?" my dad asked, pulling off his cap and running a hand through his sandy hair. I could feel his eyes on me even beneath his polarized lenses. "Is it a money thing? Lord knows, I have more than I need, and you'll get it all anyway."

"No," I said, waving a hand at him as he angled the boat around, taking it over the top of a wave as he headed into the small port area where we picked up the charters. In a few short minutes, we'd have a crowd of tourists who didn't know how to cast a line, let alone bait a hook. It was hard to complain about a job that had me working on a boat and fishing all day.

Hell, if I could drink a beer or two, it'd be ideal.

"Then what's the problem, Billy?" my dad asked as another gust of wind swept my hat off my head and ruffled my hair. It made me wish we had some sails on his custom built fifty-foot white and blue G & S. Then again, this boat had air-conditioning not only in the cabins but in the entertainment and bar area as well. Hell, it even had removable windows, so the guests could see into the cockpit of the boat while kicking back in the air-conditioning.

"There's no problem, Dad." I sighed. "Really, I'm grateful to be working with you. Not everyone gets to do this."

"Billy, I know you're not ungrateful, and truth be told, I'm really glad you're here to help me. Dealing with ten guys where none of them know what they're doing is ten kinds of difficult. You've literally dropped my workload by half." He bit his lip a bit. "So if it is money, I think we can work something out."

"Dad, it's really not about money," I said, shrugging and looking over at him. "I wish you'd stop bringing it up. If I wanted more money, I'd tell you." I touched my chest with my thumb. "Do I seem like someone who would blow smoke up your ass?"

"Not really," my dad said, scratching his bearded chin with one hand. "So, tell me what's wrong. We've got a few minutes before we're at port, so lay it on me."

"I'm bored," I said in a huff. "I mean, this place is great, and with what you pay me, I'm not really doing any worse than I was trucking when you consider I'm not on the road every night and don't pay any rent. At the same time, this is… well…"

"It's easy, eh?" He smiled, turning his eyes heavenward. "It's easy to start a job like this and look back and see twenty years have gone by." He shrugged. "There's worse things to do with one's life."

"I suppose that's true," I said, shrugging at him as the docks came into view. This was where he'd swing the boat around and back in the stall. Then we'd go up and pick up the passengers. A quick look at the docket let me know it was some kind of work retreat. The kind where someone with a corporate card was paying for everyone else on the company's dime.

I always sort of hated those trips because I hated how they threw around money that wasn't really there, but at the same time, those same guys would empty a case or two of Corona at five bucks a bottle, so it was all good.

"I think the real problem is that Mary Ann is off with that tour company," my dad said with a laugh. "No one to keep you warm at night and all that."

That was partially true. While I'd yet to make an honest woman of Mary Ann, things with her had been good. A little too good, and I knew if I stuck around much longer, I'd put a ring on it. Then I'd be stuck here, white picket fence and all, spending my days helping my dad with his charter fishing business. That would be it. We'd spend evenings at the same bars, eating fish tacos and drinking Coronas. And that was a problem because I wasn't sure I deserved it.

The deal with the Scorpions earlier in the year had cemented that fact for me. I wasn't the best guy in the world. Sure, I'd been justified in taking the drug gang out to rescue my dad, and if I had to do it again, I would, but I hardly felt like I deserved for this to be my life.

"You know, I think I wanna help people," I said, glancing at my dad. He raised an eyebrow at me as we pulled back into the spot.

"What do you mean?" he asked as I moved to grab the dock lines so I could tie us into place. "You are helping people. Hell, you're helping me right now."

"I mean really help people, Dad," I said as he ran a hand through his hair. "I was thinking about running for sheriff now that the position is open. Maybe keep what happened before from happening again. I know those kinds of people. It's only a matter of time before they realize the Scorpions are gone and this place becomes a warzone. Hell, I'm surprised it hasn't happened already."

My dad rubbed his beard again before leaning down and turning the key to cut power to the engine. "If you think that's what you need to do, Billy, I think you should." He shrugged as he came forward and grabbed the line from my hand, moving to fix my poor excuse for a knot.

"Oh, is that so?" I asked, raising an eyebrow at him.

"Yeah, I just didn't have the heart to say it." He stood up and held out his hand to me. "Don't feel like you need to find a new job just yet, but if that's what you want to do, I'm all for it."

"I'll think about it," I said, nodding at him. "Maybe talk it over with Mary Ann when she gets back."

"Good," he said before pointing toward the dock. "Now go get our customers."

2

"**D**rink up," my dad said, tossing a Corona to me as we stood next to his fishing boat, the Emerald Glimmer.

"Thanks." I caught the ice-cold beer and popped the top with my keyring while he fished his own out of the cooler. There were a lot more left than I'd expected given the long day of fishing but turns out Mr. Corporate Card had a spending limit that had been nearly exhausted by the charter itself.

"To new challenges," he said, gesturing at me with his own beer before knocking back a swig.

"And getting drunk and falling down," I said, taking a swig of mine before wiping my mouth with the back of my hand.

"Most definitely," he replied, taking down his beer in another gulp before tossing the empty into the plastic sack next to his feet. It clanged against the other empties, and I knew he'd take it home to put in the pile with the others. Then, once the pile took up too much space in the garage, he'd take it to the recycler. Hopefully, it'd be soon, otherwise I was going to do it myself.

"So, do you have to get right back home?" I asked, taking another swig of beer as I glanced around the lonely docks. It was only about five o'clock, and the sun would be up for another couple hours yet, but the place was practically empty despite being relatively close to the shops on the other side of the port. It always surprised me how the town seemed to turn into a ghost town around dinner time, but it was the type of place where people headed home after work.

"I could spare a bit," my dad replied, glancing at his wristwatch. The golden band of his knockoff Rolex glimmered in the sunlight as he turned his eyes back to me. "'Sides, the special at Malarkey's Bar and Grill is meat loaf." He stuck out his tongue, and I laughed.

"They do makes the best vegan meatloaf I've ever had," I said, finishing my Corona and offering him the bottle.

"They make the only vegan meatloaf you've

ever had, and you know what the problem with it is?" he asked, taking the bottle and bagging it before hefting the bag over one shoulder. I moved to take it from him, but he waved me off.

"What's that?" I said as he made his way toward the gate at the top of the docks.

"It doesn't have any damned meat," my dad said, patting his stomach. "You think this happens by accident? My physique requires constant attention."

I laughed as I passed by him so I could open the gate and hold it toward him. He nodded to me as he slipped through, angling toward his brand new emerald Nissan Titan. Besides my Chevy Tahoe, the truck was one of the few on this side of the lot.

He tossed the bag in the back of the truck and stood there awkwardly, and I realized that while he'd agreed to do something, we hadn't actually made plans.

"I'm really feeling like a steak after that." I gestured lamely at the boat even though I could barely see it behind the black wrought iron fence that barred the Pleasantville docks from random passersby. "I mean, fish is great and all, but I'm more of a 'red meat and beer' kind of guy. Can't help it."

"Spoken like a true Ryder, Billy-boy." My dad beamed at me. "You can tell me the truth though, son. You wanna go to Salty's but don't wanna go alone." He smiled at me as he came over and clapped me on the shoulder with one hand. "But fear not because I will happily let you buy me a steak." He removed his hand and rubbed his chin. "Say, what's on tap there right now?"

"Do you actually care?" I asked, raising an eyebrow at him as we made our way toward the entrance to the promenade. "You almost never drink anything but Corona."

"I have been known to enjoy a craft libation from time to time," he replied as we stepped onto the wooden deck of the promenade. Despite the damage that had happened earlier in the year, it'd been rebuilt, and now the shops that had survived the downtime were open.

It was always a bit amazing to me how you could see all the boats moored in the bay and smell the salty air while still seeing all the comforts of modern life. The city had done a good job of making sure the promenade had been tasteful.

The middle of the square only a few yards away was dominated by a fountain that shot streams of water into the air every half hour. In the center stood a statue of Poseidon, his trident raised triumphantly in the air while mermaids clung to his legs and stared longingly up at him. Bushes filled with assorted pink, orange, and yellow flowers blocked off the street from view, creating a natural ambiance for the stone benches surrounding the fountain.

As we moved past, a local street artist I'd come to know as Big Nick stood in the center of a huge crowd. He was a massive six and a foot tall black man who had to weigh over three hundred pounds, and like usual, he was wearing a red and white striped suit that reminded me of Dick van Dyke in *Mary Poppins*. His straw hat sat by his feet practically overflowing with bills. It must have been a good day.

"You know what I always hate about coloring books?" he asked as he leaned affectionately on his wooden cane and held up said coloring book, displaying the pages to the crowd. "The lack of colored people in it." He began flipping through it in earnest. "Not a singled colored person to be found." He sighed loudly.

I sniggered, turning away from him to look at the assortment of shops spread out along the promenade. The closest was a local wine bar that boasted the finest wines Florida had to offer along with a few it didn't. It was a nice place because the front walk looked directly out over the blue oceans, and at sunset, there was nothing quite like sitting out there and drinking a bottle of wine.

As we passed by it, I began to miss Mary Ann fiercely. She'd already been gone almost a week, and while I knew she'd be back in only a few more days, it seemed like it had been forever.

"I always like that joke," my dad said, shoving his hands in his pockets. "It's funny because, you know, it's a coloring book."

"It's a lot less funny when you explain it to me every time," I said, glancing at him. Just behind him was a bit of scarred earth from when the Scorpions had blown up the place. It hadn't been my fault, but I still felt responsible, which was one of the reasons I tried to spend money down here as often as possible.

Still, I needn't have bothered. The foot traffic, especially during good weather, was enough to bring the promenade back up to speed in a hurry. Kids ran back and forth, chasing each other with the wooden swords sold by Barnacle Dan's Authentic Pirate Booty, which also sold quite inauthentic kites, balloons, and virtually every other knickknack you could ever want. It was sandwiched between a T-shirt shop selling "I heart Pleasantville" T-shirts, and a bait shop that actually operated as a bait shop.

If you wanted to go fishing, you just had to hand them a credit card, and they'd supply you with everything. Hell, you could even go back behind the shop and fish off their "exclusive" pier.

I'd done it once or twice, but only for fun since I almost never caught anything. No, usually when I came down here it was to go to Salty's. The restaurant had been at the edge of the promenade since I was a little kid and had dark wooden walls that reminded me of a shack. Steel caricatures of fish were nailed to the walls, but the thing most incredible about the place was the pie. It was one of the things I'd missed most about Pleasantville, and since I'd come back, I'd gained a few pounds.

The thing was, I did sort of feel silly coming in to eat by myself, and with Mary Ann working on that cruise ship, I didn't fancy going home with dad just to watch him drink Corona in his underwear.

A moment later, we stepped through the restaurant's thick wooden doors. I was greeted by the sight of a thousand posters on the walls. It was always interesting because right between a picture of Joe DiMaggio swinging for the fences and a movie poster for *Some Like It Hot* was a painting of dogs playing poker. The whole place was like that, actually, covered from head to toe in pictures, posters, and everything in between.

The smells of deep pit barbecue hit my nose as we stepped up to the counter where an older lady with red hair smiled up at us. She wore a uniform that consisted of blue jeans, cowboy boots, and a blue shirt with the Salty's yellow half-moon and shaker of salt logo emblazoned on the left breast.

"Hey, Loraine," my dad called from beside me as he threw one hand up in a casual wave. "How are the kids?"

"Terrors," she said, grabbing two laminated menus out of the basket as she circled the lacquered wooden hostess's station and came toward us. "But I love 'em all the same." She looked us both up and down. "Two?"

"Yep, just the boys," I said, knocking my dad on the shoulder with one fist.

"You I can understand since Mary Ann is out of town." She grinned at me as her gaze swept over to my dad. "Him is why I worry. Didn't your doctor tell you to lay off the red meat?"

"Caught me red-handed," he said, sheepishly looking at the ground. "You won't tell, will you?"

"I haven't decided," she said as she spun on her heel and made her way through the tables. The place was a bit over half full, but I knew that in another hour or so, it'd be packed with a huge wait. The key was getting there before five thirty for two reasons. For one, you could actually get a table, and for two, happy hour ended at six.

"Man, maybe I should have just gone to Malarkey's after all..." my dad said, glancing over at me as I followed behind Loraine. She gestured to a booth in the back corner, and when I nodded, she laid the menus down on it. Then she fished a napkin wrapped fork and knife combo out of her black belt satchel and tossed them on the counter.

"Hey, it wasn't like I had to twist your arm," I said, sliding into the booth. It felt good, familiar, and I knew that if nothing changed, I'd be eating here for the rest of my life. The idea was both comforting and horrifying.

"Ken will be with you shortly, but I can grab you a drink if you like. You want the usual, Billy?" Loraine asked, glancing over at me as my dad sat down in the booth across from me.

"Sure," I said before gesturing at my dad. "And

whatever he wants too. Something tells me buying him a drink is the least I could do."

"It is the least you could do," he said, glancing at the menu for a second. "I'd ask what's on tap, but…"

"But you just want a Corona." Lorain shot him a grin. "I may have been born yesterday, but I'd have to be daft to forget you only drink Corona." She stuck out her tongue. "Can't stand the stuff myself. Give me a good nutty ale anytime." She spun on her heel to make her way back to her station so she could put in an order for our drinks.

"I dunno what she's talking about," my dad said, fingering his menu. "Try going out on a boat all day and then wanting something dark. That's just crazy. Corona is the perfect combination of refreshing and taste." He dropped his menu. "And if you add a lime, it even has vitamins. It's literally the perfect drink."

"I'm still surprised you switched to it from Miller Lite," I said, dropping my own menu. I didn't even know why I was looking because I always got the same thing. A T-bone with baked potato and broccoli. I had no idea how Salty did it back there, but the meat would literally fall off the bone, and its tenderness was only rivaled by its taste.

"Look, I don't want to argue about it," my dad said, picking up his menu again and looking it over. "Maybe I'll get a burger…"

"You say that every damned time and you never get it because you don't eat carbs. We both know you're going to get the ribs."

"I like the ribs," he countered, eyeing me over the top of the menu.

"That's fine, but I think the burger is starting to feel a bit led on," I replied as Loraine appeared with our drinks. She set the Corona in front of my dad before setting a tall house blonde in front of me. It had just the right amount of foam, and as I stared at the rivulets of condensation dripping down the frosty glass, I licked my lips.

"Thanks," my dad said, grabbing the lime from the top of his drink and squeezing it into the drink before shoving the entirety of it into the longneck.

"Remember that when you tip," she replied, smiling brightly before returning to her station.

"I will," my dad said to as he very carefully plugged the top of the beer bottle with his thumb. Satisfied, he slowly turned the beer upside down until the entire thing was upended and the lime was at the bottom of the bottle. He waited for a three count before slowly righting the bottle and removing his thumb. The beer fizzed a little, but not much and he held his bottle up. "I'm really glad you're back, Billy."

"Thanks," I said, raising my own beer. We clinked our drinks, and I took a long swig hoping I could do just that.

"There's something I've been wanting to give you," he said after a moment as he shifted uncomfortably in his seat. Then he reached into his pocket and pulled out an old-fashioned diamond ring. He slid it across the table toward me.

"Dad," I said, glancing from my mother's wedding ring to him and back again. "That's Mom's ring. Why are you giving it to me?"

"Look, Billy, I may be old, but I'm not dumb." He stared at the ring as he spoke. "I can see the way you and Mary Ann look at each other, and well, I don't want to presume or push you into something you're not ready for, but I want you to have it for when the time comes, okay?"

"Dad…"

"I think your mother would want it this way." He looked up at me and wiped his eyes with the back of one hand. "She always liked Mary Ann. She'd like for her to have this."

As I glanced down at the ring, I knew my dad was right. My mom would want Mary Ann to have the ring, but at the same time, I wasn't sure if I was ready for her to have it. I hadn't earned that. Not yet anyway.

"I..."

"Take the ring, Billy." My dad pushed the ring into my hand and closed his fingers around it. "Make an old man happy."

"Fine," I said, nodding to him.

"Good," he said. "And I wouldn't wait too long with that, either, Billy. 'Cause a girl like that will come to her senses eventually."

"Let's hope that never happens," I replied, pocketing the ring.

"Let's," he replied, clinking my glass with his bottle.

3

I rolled up to my dad's place and unlocked the gate. Shoving my way past the overgrown azaleas, I looked around the front walk. It'd been a nightmare to get the place repaired after the Scorpions had shot it up. Still, thanks to some hard working contractors, a lot of paint and elbowgrease, and more than a few choice swear words, my childhood house was nearly better than it had ever been.

As I made my way toward the door, I marveled at how the new rose bushes had blossomed, filling the air with perfume. My mother would have loved it if she were still alive.

Maybe that was why dad had planted them, but then again, he'd made Mary Ann pick out most of the flowers, so maybe she just shared the same tastes as my mom.

The front light was on even though it wasn't dark which meant my dad had flipped it on before he'd left in the morning. I'd tried to get him to set motion lights or ones that at least sensed the daylight, but he'd had none of it.

As I approached the house, it felt sort of lonely and empty because my dad had ditched me after dinner to go to Malarkey's. He'd invited me to come with him, but I'd refused because I was tired after having been in the sun all day. Worse, I had to be out there before sunrise tomorrow because we had more clients. No, it was time for this old Marine to get some shut eye.

With that in mind, I used my Mickey Mouse key to unlock the door and let myself inside. I flipped on the switch by the door, filling the living room with that fake light I always hated. Unlike the outside of the house, the inside hadn't really gotten as patched up as it should have been. Sure, the holes had been patched and repainted, but since there hadn't actually been a lot of damage to the interior, the job hadn't been as thorough. Worse since the shelves were filled with my deceased mother's knickknacks, my dad hadn't wanted to throw away the ones that had been broken, opting to keep the pieces in the places they'd once occupied.

It was a fight I hadn't wanted to have, especially since my dad was as stubborn as a mule. If he wanted to hang onto the broken pieces of china dolls and whatnot, he could.

I padded across the new green carpet, pausing long enough to flip on the overhead fan on my way to the kitchen. This was the one room that had been nearly remodeled since it had required a new doorframe and wall after it'd gotten shot up. Fresh seafoam blue paint decorated with my mom's ancient cast iron skillets stared back at me as I pulled out a Corona from the brand new chrome fridge.

As I popped the top on the beer, I moved back to the living room. I kicked off my shoes before flopping down on the new leather couch. I took a sip of the Corona, letting the carbonation roll over my tongue as I grabbed the remote and flipped on the television. It was sixty-inches and also brand new. I guess that was the key to everything. When drug dealers shoot up your house, if you live through it, the insurance companies will buy you new stuff.

The screen lit up with a news story, and as I moved to change the channel so I could find something more interesting, my phone rang. I glanced at it, and was surprised to find Ren calling me. He never called me.

I hit the mute button for the television as I answered the phone. "Hello?"

"Billy, have you seen the news?" Ren huffed breathlessly in my ear.

"No? What's up? You sound worried," I said, glancing back at the television. There was a boat on screen, but not very big. Maybe twenty feet at the outside. The kind of thing a small crew might take for a pleasure cruise around the Florida Keys.

"Are you seeing the story about the news? It's on practically every channel," his voice had ratcheted up a notch, and I could feel the anxiety leaking through his end of the phone.

I glanced back at the screen as subtitles spilled across the bottom of the television.

"The latest disappearance in a string of abductions, the Jamaican Wave has disappeared. So far no trace of the boat or its crew has been found."

"Yeah, I see it, Ren. Some kind of abduction…?"

"My daughter was on that boat, Billy!"

My blood ran cold as the beer bottle in my hand slipped from my grip, hitting the table and spilling everywhere. I leapt to my feet, taking a step closer as I hit the volume up button on the remote, sure I'd heard Ren wrong.

"This is the fifth in a string of tourist disappearances, and the Jamaican police have no leads."

"Wait, Ren, are you saying your daughter's been abducted?" I asked, hoping it wasn't true.

"Yes!" he swallowed once, twice, three times. "You have to help me find her, Billy… I don't know what else to do."

I shut my eyes for a second, thinking it through. I wanted to help him. Ren was my friend, and what's more, he'd dropped everything to help me six months ago when my dad had gone missing. He'd been there when I'd taken on the Scorpions, and I owe him.

"Jesus, Ren. I can try, maybe…" I said. "What do you know?"

"My daughter Annabeth and her friend Samantha were taking the Jamaican Wave around the keys for Spring Break." He took a deep breath. "There'd been some disappearances, but she wouldn't listen to my objections and you know how it is. What my daughter wants, she gets…" His voice cracked. "All the boats that have been targeted are boats like the Jamaican Wave. You know, the kind with young women running around in bikinis. No ransom notes, no nothing to find."

"You seem to think that's of particular interest, Ren. Why is that?" I asked, moving back through the house and heading to my room. I hastily started grabbing things and shoving them in my duffel.

"There's a major Albanian gang out there that deals heavily in prostitution, drugs, and everything else. Usually, they do simple stuff like follow girls to their hotels and abduct them." He sighed into the phone. "But this has their M.O. all over it."

"How long have they been gone? And how long do you think we have?" I asked, slinging the bag over my shoulder as I headed toward the front door. I wasn't sure exactly what was going on, but I knew one thing. I needed to get to Jamaica before the window closed. I could figure out the rest on the way.

"I'm not sure when they got abducted. Sometime in the last day because she called me last night." He took a deep breath. "Assuming they haven't killed her outright? A day or two? She'll probably be dead or sold somewhere…" Ren's voice trailed off, and I tried to push the horror of his

words out of my mind. If they didn't want her to
sell, they'd likely have already killed her.

"Okay, Ren. Calm down. I'm going to head to
Jamaica right now," I said, pushing open the door
and making my way to my Tahoe. "I need a flight.
Can you handle that?" I slung my bag into the
Tahoe before sliding into the seat.

"Yeah, I… I'll take care of it," he said. "Just
head to Miami International. I'll even got you a
hotel room there…"

"Thanks," I said, starting the Tahoe and taking
off in a squeal of burning rubber. Miami
International wasn't that far, and at this time of
night, I'd make it there pretty quickly.

"No. Thank you, Billy. There's one more
thing…" Ren took a deep breath. "I think you need
to call Max."

"I can handle things myself—"

"Billy!" Ren cried, cutting me off. "This is my
daughter we're talking about. Get help, bring her
back. Please. For me. Just call Max. Tell him I'll
owe him."

"Fine," I said because he was right. If something happened to his daughter because I hadn't
asked Max for help, I didn't know what I'd do. "I'll
call Max."

"Good," Ren replied, relief evident in his voice. "Now, let me get to work. I've got some other people I want to shake down for information. I'll call you when I have anything else, and I'll email you the confirmation for the plane and hotel. I owe you."

He clicked off before I could respond, but he was wrong, I owed him. The thing was, I'd have gone anyway.

I fiddled with the phone until I found Max's contact information. I hit the button, and it rang three times before he picked up.

"How's it going, Billy?" he asked, and I could hear an explosion in the background.

"What is all that noise?" I replied. "Did I call at a bad time?"

"I am kind of busy," Max said, and I could practically hear him shrug over the phone. "Do you need something, Billy?"

"Kind of busy doing what?" I said as I swerved around a Ford Fiesta and pulled onto the road that led out of town.

"It's part of the job, and I like blowing things up. You know what I'm about. Do you really want to have this conversation? Because, let me tell you, it's better for both of us if we don't." Max was running now. I could tell because his breathing had changed and Max was never one for cardio.

"No, I don't," I said, trying to keep the anger and desperation from my voice and failing miserably. "Ren's daughter Annabeth was on a boat with one of her friends and got abducted by pirates. I'm on the way to Jamaica to find her…" I took a deep breath. "Ren said I should call you and ask for your help."

For a long time, the only sound on the other end of the phone was Max breathing. Every breath seemed to grow louder and louder until each one beat against my brain like a bass drum.

"That's because I wouldn't have answered if he had," Max said. "Family is important though, so I can see why he asked you to talk to me. I can be in Jamaica in about a day."

"Thanks, buddy," I said into the phone. "Max. I owe you one."

"No, you don't. Ren owes me one," he replied, and I could have sworn there was gunfire in the background. "I'll give you a call when I get there, but I'm a bit busy at the moment, so if you wouldn't mind, I have things to do."

"Nope, do your thing. I'll be on a flight out, so if I don't answer, just assume my phone is off," I said.

"Good. I'll coordinate with Ren," he said and clicked off the phone.

4

I t was a little after five in the morning when I stepped off the plane in Sangster International in Montego Bay, Jamaica. I was tired but thankful I'd managed to catch a few hours of sleep at both the airport and on the plane ride. Part of me was surprised I'd slept given what was going on, but if the Marines had taught me anything, it was how to sleep when the opportunity presented itself.

Still, as I finished up with customs and moved into the crowded airport, glad I hadn't had any checked baggage because that would have made the ordeal at least twice as long. The airport itself was well kept despite the hustle and bustle even at this early hour. The heat and humidity already were permeating the air, letting me know it would get a lot worse with each passing hour.

I could hear the cries of taxis desperate to get patrons even before I stepped through the automatic glass doors and out onto the street. I hoisted my duffel on my shoulder and stepped outside.

The sunlight was blinding, and as I took in the cloudless, clear blue sky, I instinctively raised one hand to shield my eyes from the glare. A massive palm tree dominated a grassy expanse with a stone fountain. Beyond it stretched a road filled with buses and taxis, desperately trying to get patrons. The right side was cordoned off for the larger resorts, complete with separate staff in distinctive uniforms.

Beyond the road, lush vegetation filled the horizon, practically blocking all signs of civilization from view. As I sucked in a breath that smelled crisp and clean despite the congestion of the airport, I flipped out my phone to see if Ren had gotten back to me. Unfortunately, there were no messages either.

Part of me wanted to call him, but I knew it was pointless. If he had information, he'd have sent it to me. A sigh escaped me. No, that call would end with him telling me to go have a Red Stripe and wait. Only, I didn't want to wait. I wanted to do something, needed to do something because, with every second that passed, I became less likely to find Annabeth. Waiting just wasn't an option.

I glanced back around as I fished out my sunglasses, a pair of black Maui Jims. They cut down the harsh glare of the sun but didn't help me find anyone in particular. There had to be something I could do. I just wasn't sure what it was.

Only, maybe I didn't need a plan, per se. Maybe, I already knew enough to start. I moved toward the line of taxi cabs waiting by the curb and stepped up to the front. A tall, lanky man with skin like dark chocolate and a tangle of dreadlocks waved at me.

"Hey, man, you need a ride? I give you a good price." He peered at me through the rolled down passenger's window as he spoke.

"Yeah, take me to the closest bar," I said, opening the back door and throwing my bag inside. Part of me wanted to head to the Jamaican Moon Resort where I had a reservation, but given that my check-in time wasn't until three PM, I knew that would be a waste of time. No, I had other plans.

"Sure thing, boss," the guy said, turning on the car as I slid into the back along with my bag and shut the door. Hanging from the seat was a card with his name and other assorted information. "Anything you want in particular, or is it driver's choice?"

"Somewhere where I can find some horizontal entertainment, if you know what I mean," I replied, and my words caused him to peer at me in the rearview once more, though his yellow sunglasses hid his eyes from view.

"I think I'm hearing what you're putting down, sir, but this really isn't the kind of place for that." He looked back toward the road as he shifted the car into gear and took off, ambling down the road toward our destination. "Lots of bad things happen to people there. You sure you don't want to go to a rock club? Probably get you what you want, and it's a lot safer."

"I've got a few hours to kill," I said, meeting his eyes in the rearview as he looked back at me. "If you don't know how to get me what I want, that's okay. I'll just find someone else…"

"Hey, man. I didn't say that. Ole Jacob knows where to find what you want. Just tryin' to give you a friendly bit of advice." He turned his gaze back to the road and swerved around a gray van without so much as a horn blast. "If that's what you want, I know where to get you."

I stared out the window as he drove, the scenery passing by in a blur of color. I hadn't been to Jamaica in a long time, and I was surprised at how much the scenery changed. While there were still the old fashioned looking buildings, and pink stone houses lining the countryside, there were now massive skyscrapers, gates, and way more traffic than I remembered. It didn't take long to realize how much the resorts had changed things, and part of me wasn't sure it was for the better.

Still, as we pulled into a janky strip mall with a donut shop on one end, a laundromat in the middle, and a bar on the far end, I figured I was where we needed to be because very few places would have girls in that style of dress out front at five in the morning. Granted, there was only a pair of them, but that was enough to let me know Jacob had done me right. Or, well, right enough.

I nodded to Jacob, tossed him a twenty, and stepped out of the taxi. I had barely gotten my duffel up on my shoulder before he was tearing ass out of the parking lot like he desperately didn't want to be here. That was fine though. I didn't need him here for what was about to happen.

I took a deep breath and focused on the bar. Part of me wished I had a gun, but I hadn't wanted to risk it causing me problems. Only now, looking at the shadowy concrete block in front of me, I was suddenly apprehensive. If this didn't work, I might cause a lot of trouble and get nothing out of it.

Only, I couldn't think like that. This would work. I nodded to myself as I crossed the parking lot and moved toward the door. The two girls called out to me as I ducked inside, but as the filthy wooden door swung closed behind me, they turned back toward the street.

As I stepped into the dimly lit bar, I found myself staring at a smattering of tables, and a tiny bar that had been shoved in the corner like an afterthought. The rest of the room had been cordoned off by a sun-bleached curtain. An ancient lady stared at me from behind the counter, face covered in so much makeup, it was difficult to guess her actual age.

She wore a tight dress that barely seemed to keep her enormous chest and hips contained. The lady waddled toward me, huge breasts bouncing with every step.

"Are you looking for some company?" she

asked, showing me a thin smile that didn't come anywhere near reaching her eyes.

"I am looking for a bit of company, actually," I said, moving toward the bar and flopping down onto a red vinyl barstool. I dropped the duffel beside me as I stared up at the woman. Behind her was a litany of specials listed on a chalkboard, but none of them seemed particularly untoward.

The woman nodded knowingly and shrugged. "Not much to choose from around here, I'm afraid. What you see is what you get." She gestured vaguely toward the door. "Too early really." She moved back behind the cover of her small rotating fan. "You should come back later. The selection will be much better."

"Maybe you can help me out anyway," I said, pulling a hundred from my pocket and slapping it down on the bar. "Because I'm looking for something decidedly more foreign."

The lady stood there, mouth half open as she eyed me warily. "Just what are you after?" she said very carefully. "Because I'm starting to think the best thing for both of us might be for you to turn around and walk right back out the door. Then things won't have to get uncomfortable."

"Look," I said, tapping the bill with my index

finger. "That boat that went missing, the Jamaican Wave? My friend was on it. I *know* that the Albanians hit it, so all you need to do is tell me where I can find them. You keep the money, and I walk out of here. It's a win, win situation." I stared straight at her. "Or we go with option two where you will still tell me, but it will be a lot less profitable."

She looked at me for a long time, fear flashing through her eyes before she glanced around. Only there was no one here to help her.

"Are you threatening me?" she asked, taking a step backward until she was pressed against the wall behind her. "Because that wouldn't be smart." Her head jerked pointedly to a door on the side.

"Is whoever's in there going to help me?" I asked with a shrug. "Because if so, you should call them out here." I pushed the bill further. "Or you just help me, and I leave. Simple, clean, easy."

"I can give you one name only." She moved closer and leaned across the bar, one of her hands snaking out to pull the bill away. I kept it pinned to the bar with my finger.

"What's the name?" I asked, raising an eyebrow at her as she tried to pull the bill away.

"The place you want is called La Cabana de Jamaica. Clever I know." She snorted, shaking her head. "Run by a guy named Alphonse. He's a real number, trust me on that, but he can tell you a lot more than I can." I let go of the bill and she took it and stuffed it into her bra. "Now go." I nodded and moved to get up.

"Anything else I should know?" I asked over my shoulder as I headed to the door.

"Try going a bit later in the day." She pointed at the big clock on the wall behind her. "Maybe around ten. We're on island time here after all."

"Thanks," I said, glancing at my watch. I had a few hours to kill until then. Best make good use of them. After all, Ren's daughter was counting on me.

s I paced around my hotel room, my cellphone rang and rang and rang before going to voicemail. "Hello, you've reached Ren. Please leave me a message, and I'll get back to you as soon as possible." The phone beeped.

"Goddammit, Ren. Why haven't you gotten back to me? Even if you have no information, please call me." I exhaled into the phone. "Please." I clicked the phone off and stared at it. Ren should have called me by now. It was his daughter after all.

Only he didn't, and as I stood there in my hotel room staring at my phone like an idiot wondering why he hadn't given the circumstances, a minute went by, then two, then ten. I shook it off and tossed the phone on the bed, trying to ignore the sinking feeling swelling in my gut that something might be wrong.

If Ren didn't call soon, I was going to be pissed. I looked around the bland room with its bed and lone dresser before staring at my stuff, still packed away. Should I put it away? Maybe that'd give me something to do?

Part of the reason I'd come to the resort was to kill time, and I'd been sort of surprised the room had been ready when I showed up, but it seemed they knew what time my flight was coming in and had adjusted accordingly.

Staying here by myself in my room wasn't helping things since with every minute that went by I felt Annabeth slipping through my fingers. Worse, it was barely half past eight. At this rate, I was going to go insane by the time it got late enough to visit La Cabana de Jamaica.

Annoyed, I sat on the bed of my crummy hotel room. It had probably been nice when it'd been built thirty years ago, but unfortunately, it had probably been that long since someone had even thought about doing any kind of renovation and it showed.

It probably got away with it because it was so close to the beach, the sand was practically outside the window, but that didn't exactly help me now that I was sitting here practically bouncing off the pink cement walls.

Like many of the Jamaican buildings, the hotel had cement walls designed to withstand hurricanes, and while they'd made the building seem sturdy when I'd checked in, right now, they made the tiny hotel room feel claustrophobic.

I swallowed and looked at the window, watching the pale green curtain flap in the nearly non-existent breeze before flipping on the television. I tried channel surfing but couldn't focus on it well enough for it to be more than noise. My thoughts kept drifting to Mary Ann. I hadn't even told her I was here… Maybe I should? Only she'd worry about me. Still, we were in a relationship, and that meant she should know.

Reluctantly, I pulled out my phone and called her. It rang a few times before she picked up.

"Billy! How are you?" she asked, voice beaming through the phone in a way that made my heart sing. "You don't usually call this early…"

"Yeah, about that," I said, taking a long breath. "I'm in Jamaica, so I may not be able to call for a bit."

"Um… why?" she asked, voice taking on a

dangerous edge. "You know I get back home tomorrow…"

"That's the thing," I said, rubbing the back of my neck with one hand. "It's Ren. His daughter got kidnapped and we think she might be here, so I came to help find her."

Mary Ann was quiet for a long time. "Then I'm coming to help. Once we get in, I'll fly straight there."

"No!" I barked, a surge of protective anger welling up inside me. "You could get hurt. I can't have you come."

"What if you get hurt, Billy? What about that?" she asked, angry too. "I couldn't stand that thought."

"That's why I need you to stay safe." I nodded at the phone even though she couldn't see it.

"Billy, you'll need help, and last I checked Ren wasn't exactly, well, good for more than sitting behind a computer." I could hear her moving about her room on the cruise liner in a flurry of activity. "Let me get off at the port today. I can catch a plane…"

"Mary Ann, please don't." I took a deep breath and tried to be calm. "Hear me when I say I don't want you to come."

"Billy…" she paused for a long time. "Who will help you, keep you safe?"

"Max is coming. I already spoke to him." As I said the words the line got dead quiet.

"He scares me, Billy," she said after a moment. "But he's really coming? He and Ren didn't seem to get along when he came by with that girl of his. Vicky?"

"He's still coming, Mary Ann," I said, thinking back to the argument the three of them had that night we'd all gotten together in Miami. It wasn't that odd, in and of itself, since Ren and Vicky had never gotten along.

"I am too," she said, and before I could respond, the phone clicked off.

"Goddammit!" I cried, calling her back, but it just rang and rang before going to voicemail. A surge of anger ripped through me as I clenched my fist around the phone. The absolute last thing I needed was for Mary Ann to show up and get hurt. It was one thing for me to come out here for Ren, but quite another for her to do it because while I was willing to risk myself, I wasn't willing to risk her. Not even a little.

I took a deep breath, glancing at my watch and trying to calm down, but it didn't work. If I'd been bouncing off the walls before, I was going absolutely stir crazy now. Sure, I'd wanted to find Annabeth, but now I really wanted to find her before Mary Ann showed up.

"I need to get out of here," I mumbled to myself and glanced at my phone once more. "You can never do too much reconnaissance," I mumbled, shutting off the television and getting to my feet.

As I grabbed my fishing hat and shoved it on my head, there was a knock at the door. Startled, I turned toward it and stared at it for a long moment.

"Well, that's odd," I mumbled. Part of me wished I had a weapon of some sort, but at the same time, this was probably nothing. For one, no one knew I was here, and for two, it was probably just housekeeping.

"Who is it?" I called, moving a bit closer to the door.

"Housekeeping," came the muffled reply from the other side of the door. "Is it a bad time?"

"No, give me a second," I replied, trying to push my paranoia and nerves out of my head, I moved toward the door, gripped the knob, and pulled the door open. "Hello—"

My words were cut off as a man smiled at me

from the hallway. His metal teeth flashed in the bright sunlight outside as his hand shot out, clamping over my lips. My face exploded with pain as he shoved me backward and stepped through my doorway. Then he shut the door behind himself with his free hand.

"I wouldn't make any noise," he said, squeezing my jaw so hard I was sure it was going to snap in half. "You'll have plenty of time for that in a minute." He leaned in close, and the smell of rum on his breath was so thick I nearly gagged. "I like it when they squeal and beg." His tongue snaked out, scraping over his lips.

He flung me backward. The center of my back hit the bed hard. Stars flashed before my eyes as I collapsed forward onto my hands and knees. The big man took a step forward, looming over me like an angry gorilla. Prison tattoos covered his bare arms as he clucked his tongue.

"I'm not sure why you're snooping around, and I don't really care." He touched his chest with his thumb. "My job is simple. To make problems go away. You are most definitely a problem." He gripped his belt with one ebony hand. "We can do this the easy way or the hard way." He grinned, taking a step closer so his crotch pressed against my face. "Part of me hopes you'll choose the hard way."

I shook my head, trying to orient myself while the big man stared at me with cold, flat eyes, blocking any hope of escape with his massive body.

"So that's how this is gonna be?" I asked, and as I reached out to push him away, he jerked me forward by my hair. White hot pain flashed across my scalp as the big man ground my face against the front of his jeans.

"I can, and I will," he said, an undertone of pleasure filling his voice. "And there's nothing you can do to stop me."

I shut my eyes and sucked in a quick breath right before the big man decked me, knocking me flat on my back and creating some much-needed space between us. As I lay there, he stood over me and shook his head.

"Get ready to meet your maker," He jerked off his belt and snapped it between his hands.

As he lashed out with the buckle, I rolled to the side. It struck the tile next to me with a crack as I scrambled to my feet. His eyes narrowed in anger, and as he shifted to swing at me again, I threw myself forward. My shoulder slammed into his gut, knocking him off his feet and sending us both crashing to the ground. My shoulder drove the breath from his lungs in a whoosh, and his head cracked against the tile.

"Tell me where to find the Jamaican Wave!" I snarled, rearing back and decking him in the face. My blow shattered his nose, and as blood sprayed from the wound, I moved to hit him again. My next blow stunned him enough for me to leap to my feet. I scrambled across the room and grabbed his fallen belt as he rolled onto his hands and knees. Before he could get up, I kicked him in the stomach.

He cried out in pain, flopping onto his side, cradling his abdomen as blood poured from his ruined nose.

"I'm gonna ask again," I snapped, looping the belt around his throat and settling onto his back. Then I jerked hard on the belt to get his attention. "Where is the Jamaican Wave?"

I let loose a little so he could speak, but instead of answering, his hands snaked up, trying to loop around the belt and pull it free. His eyes bugged out of his skull as reared back and yanked on the belt wrapped around his neck. I twisted, using my shoulder for leverage. It took about ten seconds for the man's movements to slow to a stop.

Part of me wanted to keep tightening the noose,

to choke the life out of him for attacking me and being part of whatever this was, but I couldn't… I needed information. I released the hold on him and leaned forward, grabbing his hair with my free hand and smashing him face first into the tile.

"Tell me where I can find the Jamaican Wave," I snarled into his ear before driving him into the tile once more. "If you do, I won't kill you." I smashed him into the tile for good measure.

"Screw you," the guy wheezed. "I ain't no snitch, and you're a dead man." He began to laugh then, a horrible sound that gurgled up from his throat. "You won't get anything from me."

Before I could stop myself, I smashed his face into the ground until he went limp. His face was a smear of bloody meat as I forced myself to release my hold on his hair. Part of me wanted to keep hitting him, to take out all my frustration on him, but that wouldn't help.

No. I needed to get out of here now. If this guy had found me here, there might be others, and while I didn't know specifically why they were here, I was betting I'd pissed someone off already. That'd make things a lot harder than it needed to be.

I approached the still ajar hotel door and peeked outside to find two more thugs dressed in wife beaters smoking against the far wall. One had a paper wrapped bottle in his hand and was way more interested in it than looking to see me. I pulled my head back inside and sighed. This wasn't going to be fun without a weapon…

Then again, maybe I had one. I made my way back toward the unconscious guy and frisked him. Sure enough, I found a 9mm Beretta 92FS tucked into his belt. Good. Now I had a weapon. I pulled it free and checked the fifteen round magazine and found it full. Satisfied, I reloaded the weapon, flipped off the safety, and pulled the slide back, slotting a round.

I stood, moved toward the doorway, and leaned heavily against the cement wall. Then I took a deep breath. I exhaled as I moved, spinning around through the doorway and firing off three quick shots. The first two rounds caught the left thug in the throat and head, blowing his brain out across the hallway. The next shot caught his friend as he turned toward me. The round took him in the chest, and he staggered backward, one hand going to his chest as I fired one last time. The shot took him in the forehead, causing the back of his head to blow out in a spray of bloody paste.

Not jogging but not walking either, I moved past

the elevators and approached the door to the stairs. My ears were ringing from the shots, and while I was willing to bet these thugs had a deal with the owners, I was also pretty sure gunshots would arouse suspicion. Even more reason for me to get out of here. It made me glad Ren had booked the room for me, and it wasn't actually linked to my name.

I shouldered open the door to the stairs and swept my gun through the opening but found no one. The stairwell was clear all the way down, but as I exited, I put my sunglasses back on and looked out into the hotel lobby. Satisfied no one was there as I looked around and took in the scenery, I tucked the gun back into my shorts, hiding it beneath my Hawaiian shirt.

"Show time," I whispered, pulling my phone out of my pocket and switching it to camera mode. Then I made my way across the lobby toward the hotel's front entrance like a stupid tourist too engrossed in picture taking to actually pay attention to my surroundings. Thankfully, the clerks at the desk were too busy dealing with the phones to pay much attention.

The moment I swung the heavy hotel doors

open, I nearly went blind despite my sunglasses. I blinked several times, but almost wished I hadn't.

Sitting on a motorcycle parked outside the hotel was another thug. Three more riderless motorcycles sat next to it, metallic blue paint sparkling in the Jamaican sunshine. As the guy turned to look at me, I saw one of his hands reach behind him. I leapt forward, crossing the distance between us in the time it took him to free his gun.

As it came around, I kicked him in the chest, sending him toppling to the ground. His gun went flying as his bike fell on top of him, and as his helmeted head bounced off the asphalt, I grabbed the bike and hauled it off of him.

"Thanks for the ride," I said, leaping on the motorcycle and kick started it. The bike roared to life, and I sent it forward into traffic amid a blast of car horns and shouting.

6

As I tore through the Jamaican streets on my stolen motorcycle, I quickly realized lanes meant nothing to Jamaican taxi drivers. I swerved narrowly avoiding a green and yellow cab that had merged into the lane in front of me. I whipped around it, barely missing its driver's side mirror.

I gunned the bike, trying to reach a break in traffic ahead. As my motorcycle roared, a giant white van filled with cackling tourists threw on its left turn signal and swerved in front of me. I hit the brakes while trying to turn out of the way as cars all around me hammered their own brakes. The sound of screeching tires and the smell of burned rubber filled my nose.

My tires skidded as I turned sharply, maneuvering the bike into a space between the van and the rusty red Nissan pickup to my left. The Nissan's door opened suddenly, smacking into the front tire of the motorcycle and sending me flying forward. My knees crashed into the top of the door as I flew, causing me to tumble to the ground.

Agony exploded through my elbows and forearms as I rolled across the asphalt. My head smacked against the pavement with a loud crack. My vision shook, and white flashed across my eyes. A cacophony of horn blasts and people screaming filled the air as I lay there stunned.

Someone grabbed me under the arms and hauled me backward toward the open doors of a tan van with the words "Super Cleaners" stenciled on the side in big, fading-green letters. I grabbed my Beretta while fighting off the pain and disorientation ripping through my body. As I was hauled backward, I angled the gun behind me and fired.

There was a cry behind me, and warm, sticky fluid spattered across the back of my neck. I fell again, but this time I threw my arms out to cushion the blow. I hit the asphalt hard on my back. Pain screamed through my hands, but I ignored it as I rolled to my knees.

A woman in combat fatigues lay on her back in

front of me, blood gushing from a bullet wound in her stomach. She had one hand on her gut, trying to staunch the blood as it flowed between her fingers while her other hand was reaching for the pistol on the ground beside her.

As her fingers grasped for the weapon, I put a bullet in her face. Brain and bone splattered the pavement as the doors to the van opened, revealing two guys dressed in combat fatigues with AK-47s.

I fired at them while leaping to the side. I hit the ground beside the Nissan as they scrambled for cover. A second later, automatic fire tore into the Nissan, chewing through the metal and ricocheting off the ground beside me.

I fired again while scrambling behind a blue Volkswagen bus. More gunfire blew apart the street, chewing an angry erratic line across where I'd been. The breath whooshing out of me as I slammed into the ground. Gunfire ripped through the air, tearing through the bus's windows and showering me with glass.

"I definitely tried to pay off the wrong girl," I grumbled, moving forward on my elbows and looking under the VW. A bullet ricocheted off the asphalt to the left of the vehicle as I pulled out my cellphone. I flipped on the camera and used the device to give myself a quick glimpse at my attacker.

Sweat poured down my face as I angled my pistol into the air and fired. The staccato crack of the gunshot filled my ears as the gunman's throat exploded in a wash of lead. He collapsed backward arms flailing. His buddy tried to fire at me, but was thrown off as his friend instinctively grabbed onto his arm.

The shots went wide, ripping into the cement building behind me. He glared at his friend, pushing him backward into the van as I returned fire. The world was instantly quiet in the wake of my shots, distilling into a low-pitched whine as my attacker slumped forward, blood gushing from his chest. His AK slipped from his hand and clattered to the ground as he collapsed in front of the van.

Something exploded to my left and heat washed over me. The tourist van flipped through the air, flame, and smoke filling the sky. I swung my head around to see a gaggle of small children crowded into an alcove of an old wooden building that looked like it hadn't been built to the current earthquake codes. What if they got hurt? What if something happened to those kids because I was out here and they got caught in the crossfire? The thought made me sick. I'd make these bastards pay for putting them in harm's way.

The van slammed into a wall upside down, shattering the front window, flaming tires spinning as black smoke leapt from it. I turned toward the direction of the attack and saw another guy clad in military fatigues leaning out of a black Jeep. He had what looked like a rocket launcher on his shoulder.

"Damn," I muttered, firing my Beretta at him as he frantically tried to reload his weapon. Bullets tore through his skull, ending his life in a puff of bone and blood that caused his body to slump forward and crash to the ground beside the Jeep. The rocket launcher clattered emptily to the pavement, the sound of it deafening despite all the noise around me and the ringing in my ears.

Part of me couldn't believe these people not only had explosives but would actually use them on a crowded street. While part of me wondered what I had stumbled into, most of me didn't care. I had to move, had to stop them, and I had to do it away from all these people.

I sidestepped a burning tire as it flew through the air and dodged to my left as a gargantuan man with long black dreadlocks and thick ugly scars crisscrossing his cheeks came at me from between two cars with a machete. The blade missed me by an inch. My foot lashed out, catching the guy in the knee with a horrific snap. He cried out before his scream was cut off by a chop to the throat with my Beretta.

His machete clattered to the floor as a bullet zipped by my ear. I dropped, grabbing the man's machete and sending it flying toward the shooter in one smooth motion. A scream that was mostly gurgling erupted from my target as the biker from the hotel staggered backward, the machete planted in his throat.

He collapsed forward onto his knees, fingers clutching at the blade as his lifeblood spurted from his neck. I took off in a run and made it three steps before machine gun fire turned the pavement beside me into rubble.

"Damn!" I cursed, darting inside a cement building full of towels, t-shirts, and other assorted swimwear.

I glanced around the store and found myself staring through the back door at a wharf. Several speedboats and other vehicles designed to be rented to tourists sat idle only a few yards away.

More gunfire erupted from outside, shattering the windows as I threw myself to the ground. I hit hard on my shoulder and rolled onto my back, firing back at my attackers. They answered back by showering the store with bullets. The big front window shattered, filling the floor with shards of razor-sharp glass.

Random spray filled the store, chewing into the concrete walls and letting me know one thing, they couldn't see me. I crawled forward on my elbows as quickly as I could until I hit the cement hallway leading out to the back door. I scrambled to my feet as I sprinted across the room.

I kicked open the flimsy metal back door, the small hook keeping it closed ripping free of the wood with a crack as the thin, white metal door slammed against the outer wall. I stood, tensed like a lion and listened with one ear cocked toward it. When no sounds erupted from the alley, used my phone to look out past the frame. No one was in sight. Nor did anyone shoot at me.

"Okay, Billy. You got this," I mumbled to myself, trying my best to ignore the old man crouching behind the register in a puddle of piss.

I darted out the door and crouched behind an old metal dumpster made more from rust than anything else. Sucking in a breath, I grabbed onto the top of the cinderblock wall and pulled myself up and over. As I moved toward the wharf, I stripped off my Hawaiian shirt and dropped it to the ground. It wasn't much of a disguise, but it was better than nothing.

Sirens cut through the air, screaming and wailing toward the street behind them as I stepped out into the next street, moving into a crowd of people that weren't moving so much as gawking at the smoke rising from the street behind them.

The police would be here in a moment, and while I wasn't sure if they were bought off, I was pretty sure they wouldn't be happy with me emptying a gun in the middle of the street, let alone all the corpses I'd just made.

As I stepped out of the crowd, and around a small cart decorated with souvenirs, I found the owner nowhere to be found. Was he part of the crowd?

I wasn't sure, but I took the opportunity to score myself a green, yellow, and red Rastafari hat. I pulled it on as I moved onto the dock and headed toward a thin black man wearing an ill-fitting black PADI T-shirt and tattered black swimming trunks.

"I want a Jet Ski," I said, pulling out a wad of bills and waving them at the man to get his attention. "Do you have any available?"

The man turned his eyes from the black smoke curling in the distance and looked from me to my handful of bills and back again. He swallowed, adam's apple bobbing up and down in his throat like a bouncing basketball at the sight of my money before shaking himself into action. "Why yes. We do have some. We can rent you one for the day." He smiled and named a price way higher than the sign to his left read.

"Thank you so much," I said, shoving a wad of bills into his hand as I took the key from him.

The man stood there dumbfounded, mouth opening and closing as I rushed down the pier and leapt on the Jet Ski he'd indicated before he had even taken half a step toward me. I started the vehicle as a burst of gunfire tore into the rental guy, flinging him backward onto the deck. Anger surged up in me as his body fell forward into the water in front of me. Those bastards had turned that poor son of a bitch into collateral damage, and for that, they'd pay.

Men wearing ski masks fired at me from across the street while sprinting toward me. Bullets zipped through the air, tearing up the dock and puncturing the warm ocean surrounding me. My jaw set in determination, and I punched the throttle. The Jet

Ski tore forward through the surf, churning the water into white foam as I zigged and zagged, bullets plunging into the sea all around me.

As the dock disappeared into a dot behind me, the telltale roar of a speedboat filled my ears.

7

My muscles strained as I spun the Jet Ski around to face the speedboat and raised my Beretta. One of the men inside had something in his hands. I sighted him and pulled the trigger, emptying the weapon. The bullets punched into his chest, and the thing in his hands slipped from his grip and disappeared into the boat.

"Dammit," I cried at the empty gun before spinning the Jet Ski around in a wide arc of churning water. As I gunned it, an explosion ripped through the air behind me, spitting debris and fire into the wind. I glanced over my shoulder to see a huge hole in the speedboat's side, flames rippling outward across its hull as it listed haphazardly to the left and revealed two more boats and a trio of Jet skis.

I gunned the throttle and shot off in a shower of foam, bounding over the waves as gunfire tore into the ocean around me. Salty spray hit me in the face while I leaned forward on the Jet Ski and ground the throttle as hard as I could. It whipped forward as I turned a hard left.

The Jet Ski went up on its side, arcing around behind the speedboats. They raced by me, leaping over the waves as they tried to turn to follow me. Only, I didn't give them time. I gunned the throttle, shooting myself forward toward the trio of Jet skis while ducking as close to the machine as I could. Bullets smacked into the Jet Ski. The engine screamed in pain, and the smell of acrid smoke filled the air as the trio bore down on me.

The spray of gunfire coming from the lead Jet Ski halted, and a quick glance let me know why. He was busy reloading his weapon, and since he was between me and the other two, his friends couldn't fire on me.

Black smoke poured from my Jet Ski, and as it coughed and wheezed, I twisted the throttle as hard as I could. Water that smelled a lot more like gasoline than it should, erupted from the back as I burst forward through the ocean.

As the leader finished reloading his MAC-10, I leapt from my dying Jet Ski. I crashed into him shoulder first and wrapped my arms around him. We tumbled off the back of his Jet Ski and crashed into the sea. His head and back slammed into the water, absorbing the majority of the impact while the two other riders burst past us. As the warm Caribbean Ocean swallowed us, he tried to bring his gun around. I drove my fist into the underside of his chin. His head snapped backward, and the gun slipped from his grip. I lunged for it, barely managing to wrap my fingers around it as my attacker recovered.

I spun underwater and fired a two-second burst. The bullets threw off streams of bubbles as they flew through the water and slammed into his chest in an upward arc. The water turned bloody red as I kicked with everything I had, hitting the surface a second later.

The other two jet skis were coming back, and behind them I could see the speedboats as well. I fired at them with my MAC-10. Bullets tore through the left one, causing him to veer off, but the right one ignored my fire, raising his own weapon.

I dove back down, using a combination of the water and the dead man to block the bullets. They slammed into his corpse as the Jet Ski got closer. I waited a hair's breadth before popping back up and emptying the Mac-10 into him at close range. The line of gunfire practically cut him in half as it threw him from the Jet Ski and into the water.

As his bloody corpse hit the ocean, I frantically ran my hands over the dead man I'd been using as a shield. My hands closed on another magazine and I jammed it in place as the left Jet Ski came back. Like before, when I shot at him, he veered off, but it almost didn't matter because the speedboats were almost here.

"Dammit!" I cried, pushing off the corpse and moving toward the closest Jet Ski where it lay sputtering in the water a few yards away. I reached it as the right speedboat opened fire, filling the ocean with lead.

"Focus, Billy," I mumbled to myself as I dove beneath the water and moved beneath the Jet Ski. I grabbed onto the side and pushed on it counter-clockwise. It spun around easily righting itself as bullets filled the water. My lungs screamed for air as the speedboats zipped by me, and as their trails cut away from me in the water, letting me know they were coming back for another pass, I turned my attention toward the last jet ski.

He was nearly on top of me. Only, I was out of options. I couldn't breathe underwater, and I was getting tired. I aimed the MAC-10 at the Jet Ski and fired, emptying the weapon into the underside of the Jet Ski, causing it to lurch violently to the right.

I wasn't sure if I'd damaged it, the rider, or both, but I didn't care. I burst from the water, sucking in a gulp of air as I hauled my ass onto the back of the Jet Ski. As I wiped the water from my eyes, I saw the speedboats were coming back.

I ground down on the throttle and the Jet Ski surged forward, much faster than mine had been. Only it didn't seem to matter. As the speedboats' engines roared, I knew they'd be within range soon. I glanced around, looking for something, anything to use as a weapon and found myself staring at a waterproof bag toward the back of the Jet Ski.

While trying to drive with one hand, I reached back to open the bag. I pulled the Velcro off and unzipped it to find myself staring at a weapons cache. There was an empty spot for a MAC-10, but there was also a Glock, two magazines and, better still, a pair of grenades.

I snatched one of the grenades, pulled the pin

and flung it backward toward the first boat. It arced through the air, not exactly on target, but what's that saying? You only have to be close in horseshoes and hand grenades? The explosive detonated right beside the left boat, blowing a hole in the bottom, left side of it and causing it to list right into the other boat. Its nose slammed into the tail of the other speedboat, ripping the motor off in a shriek of shattering fiberglass.

Before they could recover, I snatched the second grenade from the case and put the Jet Ski in a turn that had me heading toward them, I pulled the pin and flung the grenade with a lot more accuracy as I burst by them. They were way too busy with their boats to even notice me as the grenade landed inside the right speedboat.

The boom was deafening, spraying bits and pieces of speedboat, water, and debris in every direction. I didn't stop to check out the damage. Instead, I pushed the Jet Ski to the limit and shot off through the water toward a massive resort in the distance. A quick glance around didn't reveal the third Jet Ski, and while I was curious, I really didn't want to wait around for more bad guys.

8

B y the time I was a few hundred yards away
from the resort, the black smoke from the
firefight with the speedboats was just a
pale shadow of its former glory. I paused just long
enough to shove my phone into the waterproof
pocket of my shorts before diving into the ocean.
The water was surprisingly warm, reminding me of
a lukewarm bath, and what's more, the waves were
nearly nonexistent.

Kicking my feet, I swam toward the big yellow
buoys that marked the resort's roped off area and
clambered over the top of it. While the beach
wasn't empty, and the big floatation devices
anchored in the surf were filled with people, no one
gave me even a passing glance as I dropped onto
the private beach.

I moved quickly, swimming the few feet it took me to reach an area where I could stand. The white sand was rough beneath my feet, making me think it was composed largely of shells, and as I waded forward toward the beach, little fish nipped at my legs.

Hastening my pace while trying to look like I belonged here, I made my way past a young couple with a frozen, multi-colored drink in each hand. The male, an Italian guy with crazy chest hair and a huge gold chain, nodded at me as we passed.

As I stepped onto the beach and glanced around for trouble, I found none. Most of the patrons were lyying out on the white and blue pool chairs or lounging under private cabanas while butlers in full dress brought them drinks. Even more people were crowded around the two bars at the edge of the sand, fighting for attention from the brown-shirted bartenders.

Standing here, it was almost hard to believe there had been a firefight only a few miles away. Most of the people here probably didn't even know there had been an explosion across town. That was good though, it meant no one would be on the lookout for me, and besides, as I wiped my forehead with the back of one hand, I realized I looked just like any other tourists.

That was the reason I had come here. The resort would be doing its best to keep people from freaking out about a shootout in downtown. Inside these walls, everything was still fun, sun, and booze.

As I stepped past a woman in a straw hat pounding down a frosty white drink, the woman took one swaying step toward a hairy-chested man on my left and nearly stumbled into me. I side-stepped quickly and hurried past the couple, not wanting to cause a scene. Dealing with hotel security was the absolute last thing I needed right now.

They didn't seem like trouble, but that didn't mean trouble wasn't here. How hard would it have been to track my departure from the docks across town and come here? Not very hard at all.

Part of me was a little surprised at the lack of a police helicopter though. Maybe they'd treated the speedboat chase as a separate incident from the shootout outside the hotel? Still, it had to have been a lot of carnage for such a small town. Perhaps it had taken my enemies a while to get regrouped, especially given the havoc in the streets.

Knowing all that, part of me was still amazed no one had followed me. I shook the thought away and moved onto the car-lined street in front of the resort. The sight surprised me because part of me hadn't expected so many vehicles right outside since I imagined most people were bussed in. Then again, from the look of the old cars, they probably belonged to employees. Guess the resort hadn't wanted to devote any space to employee parking.

As I stepped past the cars and moved toward the street light on the corner, I realized I could still hear sirens in the distance. A sinking feeling filled my gut as I made my way down the street. Just being out here could get me caught, and what's more, they knew where my room was so I couldn't even go back and change. No, I was on my own with what I had on me and nothing else.

I quickly checked my person and breathed a sigh of relief when I found my passport and wallet still in my pocket. Thanks to my waterproof pocket, my phone was even working. I pulled it out and dialed Ren again, but like last time, it rang a few times before going to voicemail.

"Hey, Ren. There's been some trouble at the hotel. I got attacked there. Sorry. Give me a call back to discuss, okay?" I clicked off the phone and shoved it back in my pocket before making my way forward along a busy street crowded with vendors hawking everything from bead necklaces to custom artwork. The building all had the same cement walls. While they were all decorated in greens, reds, and yellows, something about them made them all look the same.

People milled about, hanging out in doorways as I moved past them all, trying my best to scan the streets for danger and ignore the people shouting at me to buy authentic spices, beer, or local medicinals.

After a few minutes, I found myself on a street toward the edge of the city. La Cabana de Jamaica stood on the corner, and while the shops on the street next to it had the same look as every other shop, the bar's walls were plastered over in a way that made it look like an old speakeasy.

The front windows were dark and reflective, making the words "La Cabana de Jamaica" stand out in the glare of the sun. There were a few tables outside filled with tank-topped tough guys playing cards and passing around rum bottles.

As I watched them from my spot beside a Cajun restaurant, I could tell they were on high alert from the way they kept glancing around like they were expecting the other shoe to drop. Worse, because their gazes kept flitting to the pair of black BMWs sitting on the curb in front of the bar, I knew it probably had to do with whoever had been in those vehicles. A quick glance at my watch revealed it to be barely half past nine. Was that why the lady at the other shop had wanted me to wait until after ten? Was it because of whoever was in those cars?

I wasn't sure, but I knew one thing, going in the front door was out. No. I needed another way. Fast.

I glanced around, trying to come up with an idea, and as I did, I found myself staring through the big front window of the ice cream stand to the left. Even from here, I could see the back wall was glass as well with a seating area outside.

"At least I'll be able to check it out from the other side," I said to myself as I ducked inside. The fans overhead spun in lazy arcs that did little to cool the room and even less to deter the mass of flies buzzing around.

A toothless old lady stared at me from behind the counter, face etched from years of sun and hard work. She was clad in a frayed sunflower yellow uniform that strained to keep her enormous bulk contained. The lady waddled toward me, huge hips sashaying as she moved, and I marveled at how the woman fit through such a narrow space so easily. Lots of practice, I supposed.

"What can I get you?" She grinned, revealing a mouthful of gums. "We have an afternoon special you might like?"

"Maybe in a bit. I'm waiting for a friend," I said, shrugging as I shuffled past the woman and out onto the outdoor patio on the other side. "When she comes in, can you guide her out here?"

The woman nodded knowingly and sighed. "Well, let me know when you're ready. Menus are on the table," she said in that, "you better buy something or leave" tone.

Instead of responding, I made my way over to the low wall separating the outdoor patio from the alleyway. I glanced back into the shop to make sure the woman wasn't watching and saw she'd moved back behind the cover of her small rotating fan.

With one quick movement, I leapt over the wall and landed on the other side. I stood there, crouched against the wall and looked around, making sure no one spotted me. Then I made my way down the gravel-filled alley toward a weather-beaten building on the corner. From the back, La Cabana de Jamaica didn't look very secure, but from what I had seen out front, I was sure it was chock full of armed men.

Walking toward the back door of La Cabana de

Jamaica, I took a deep breath. It was go time, and after what had happened at the hotel, I wasn't giving anyone the benefit of the doubt. If they were innocent, they wouldn't be there now.

I knocked on the door. There were the sounds of it unlocking, and as it started to open, I kicked it as hard as I could. There was a cry inside as something hit the ground like a sack of potatoes. I shoved the door the rest of the way open, Glock at the ready.

The only person in the kitchen was a short black woman dressed in a pink bikini top and jean short shorts. She lay sprawled next to the door, eyes rolled up in the back of her head. I stepped past her unconscious body and moved through the kitchen. As I reached the hallway, I spied a man wearing a black polo with La Cabana de Jamaica emblazoned across the chest in gold writing approaching. Only this guy was way too built and muscular to be an average waiter, even if I was willing to ignore the prison ink up and down his tanned arms.

I debated shooting him, but that'd draw too much attention so I ducked back into the kitchen and grabbed a large metal frying pan off one of the racks. As the waiter appeared, I slammed the pan into his nose. The blow snapped his head back, and he crumpled in a heap against the wall.

Before anyone could spot him, I grabbed his arm and pulled him into the kitchen and dragged him behind one of the counters. I frisked him and found a silenced Beretta and an extra magazine in a holster under his shirt. I quickly pulled the holster off the man and used his belt to wrap it around my own waist. I checked the Beretta before readying the weapon and moving forward into the hallway.

The door at the end of the hallway opened to reveal two men sitting across a card table from one another. Both were dressed in the same polos as the guy I'd hit with the frying pan, and like him, their arms were covered in similar ink.

Their shaved heads glistened in the low light of the room as they looked woozily over at me. The rum bottle between them nearly empty, and as they both put their hands on the table to try to push themselves to their feet, I fired at them. They collapsed onto the card table, knocking it to the ground and causing the rum bottle to spill all over the floor to mix with their blood.

"Hey, what's going on out there?" A voice called from behind the bathroom door on the right wall. I approached quickly and kicked the door right beside the handle as hard as I could. The jamb splintered into wooden fragments as the door burst inward and smacked against the wall to reveal another gangster sitting on the john.

"Who are you?" he asked, eyes wide as dinner plates.

"Justice," I said, pulling the trigger and decorating the bathroom wall with bloody chunks.

I spun on my heel as he slumped forward off the toilet and onto the ground. I rushed through the other doorway, heading toward the next room. As I reached the door, I heard people arguing on the other side, and I paused, listening.

"Tell Llanzo Gayle we've carefully considered his offer," a man with a gruff, angry voice said. "And we're going to pass." His words were accentuated with the whump, whump of silenced shots followed by the sound of two bodies hitting the floor amidst a crash of bottles. I wasn't sure what was happening on the other side of the door, but I was going to find out.

I nudged the door carefully open with my boot. The first thing I noticed was the smell. The scent of alcohol hit me like a punch in the face. I edged my head out, careful to keep low. A pale man dressed in a wife-beater with scraggly black stubble and a cigarette in his mouth stood over the body of an older black man in a blue polo and khaki pants with a silenced submachine gun in one hand.

The door creaked. The man turned toward me, raising his silenced submachine gun. I fired. My rounds caught him in the chest, sending him sprawling backward against the bar. His weapon slipped from his hands and hit the floor with a thud as he reached up and touched his chest.

As he stared at his bloody hand, his eyes squinted in confusion. He turned the look on me as I moved toward him.

"What happened here?" I whispered as the guy slumped to his knees beside the corpse of polo guy number one. When he didn't respond, I put the Beretta to his forehead. "I asked you a question."

"What?" he asked, blinking at me. The light was already fading from his eyes, and as he started to slide to the floor, I grabbed him by the hair.

"Never mind. Where's Alphonse? I need to ask him some questions," I said, kneeling down next to him and smacking his cheek in an effort to keep him focused on me. He was bleeding out, but he wasn't dead yet.

"Alphonse?" the guy murmured, and as he turned his head toward the bar, a shotgun blast tore through the massive mirror behind the bar, spraying buckshot and glass into the tiny room. I threw myself to the ground, landing hard on my elbows, and trained my weapon on the hole.

I crawled forward and snatched the goon's fallen submachinegun and trained it on the broken mirror. "Alphonse, if that's you, I just want to talk!" I called.

Another shotgun blast was my only reply. It tore into the spot beside me, splintering the bar and shattering glasses. I fired back.

There was a scream from behind the wall, and another shotgun blast punched a huge hole in the thin wood, closer, but nowhere near my location. I let loose another volley knee high, emptying the submachine gun before dropping it to the ground.

A scream filled my ears as I grabbed one of the bar stools and heaved it at the wall. The thin, bullet-perforated drywall caved in like tissue paper to reveal a short white guy with a shaved head. His legs were a mishmash of bone and blood, and as he looked up at me, I realized he was going into shock. He didn't have long left.

I pointed the Beretta between his eyes. "What happened to the Jamaican Wave?"

"Wh-what?" he stammered, looking from me to

the gun and back again. "What happened to Chaz?"

"He's dead. They're all dead." I pressed the barrel against his forehead, forcing his head backward against the thin wall of the room. "Now tell me about the Jamaican Wave."

"I'm going to die already. Why should I tell you?" He gestured at his legs for emphasis.

I shot him in the shoulder. "Maybe, maybe not." I leaned in close and pointed the gun at his other shoulder. "But if you don't start talking, you'll definitely die. Painfully."

"Fine." He patted his pockets. "Spare me a cigarette?"

I shot him in the other shoulder. "I feel like I may have been unclear about your options. Start talking. Now." I pointed the gun at his crotch."

"Okay!" he cried, shaking his head violently.

"Where is the Jamaican Wave?" I said, kneeling down next to him. "Tell me."

"They already got delivered to Llanzo Gayle." He sighed and smacked his chest with one hand, smearing blood across the dirty white tank top. "He's the big dog in these parts. Has a finger in every pie. He wanted some more." He flailed toward the guys in the polos. "We decided he could pound sand. The rest of our boys are on their way to visit him now." He coughed, spraying blood.

"Why does Llanzo want the girls? Where would he keep them?" I asked, trying to remain calm even though everything in me wanted to shoot the guy and go find Llanzo.

"Why not?" His eyes went a bit glassy as he shrugged.

"Stay with me," I snarled, slapping him. His eyes cleared as he looked at me. "Where would he take the girls?"

"No idea." He cracked a grin then and nodded to himself. "Seems we're after the same thing, maybe. I could help you get to Llanzo, help you find the boat."

"If I find Llanzo, I'll find the girls?" I asked, and he nodded. So Llanzo Gayle was the guy I needed to find. The man at the top.

"If he doesn't know where they are, no one will, but it'll be hard to get to him. Place is locked down…" He coughed, spraying blood across the front of his shirt. "I'd say that deserves a cigarette. Chaz will have some. Please…"

"Fair enough," I said, moving back across the room and bending over the dead Albanian on the ground. Like he'd suggested, I found a lighter and a cigarette. I tossed him the pack. It hit his chest and slid into his lap. He stared at it, and sort of flailed at it with one bloody hand, struggling to pull out a cigarette.

"Thanks," he said, nodding to me as he put the bloody cigarette to his lips. "It's funny you know, I never thought I'd end up like this."

"No one ever does," I said, handing him the lighter.

He nodded as he sucked on his cigarette and blew out a long breath. "That's very true."

"So, where can I find Llanzo?" I asked, taking the cigarette from him and tossing it to the ground beside him.

"In Hell," he said, pulling a small, black cylinder from his pocket and popping the spoon. "Whoops."

As the metal tab hit the alcohol soaked floor, I spun on my heel and sprinted toward the front of the bar. I threw myself forward, smashing through the doors of La Cabana de Jamaica as an explosion of fire and brimstone blew the room out across the Jamaican street.

The building swayed, listing toward the damaged wall and partially collapsing as the shock-wave threw me into a parked car. I lay there, ears ringing because my hearing had been reduced to a dull warble as dust and debris filled my vision. The far-off cry of sirens filled my ears, but I couldn't trust my hearing well enough to tell how close they might be.

As flames leapt from the bar's partially caved-in roof so it resembled a funeral pyre, I climbed slowly to my feet. I felt woozy from the blow, but thankfully, I was mostly in one piece. I moved quickly, angling to blend into the crowd, and saw the old lady from the ice cream shop standing outside, gaping at the demolished bar.

"What happened?" I asked, catching her eye and pointing at the black smoke in the sky. "I heard a huge explosion…"

The woman looked at me, fear flashing across her face before she shook herself. "Drug war," she murmured. "Today is the day Llanzo Gayle collects his tribute around the island." She looked around the street. "You should get out of here before things get worse," she added before hurrying back inside her shop and switching the sign in the window to closed.

"If you only knew," I replied, making my way down the street as sirens split the air. Part of me was annoyed I hadn't gotten there a few minutes earlier.

If I had, I could have gotten one of Llanzo Gayle's tax collectors. It would have saved me a lot of trouble because I didn't know exactly where Llanzo Gayle was.

I took one last look around before swiping a red and green t-shirt with a picture of Bob Marley on it from an unattended rack, the shop's owner having disappeared into the crowd of onlookers gawking at the explosion. In one quick movement, I pulled on the new one. After another step, I snatched a gray canvas fishing cap and pulled it on.

Police cars and fire engines zoomed by as I turned the corner and walked out of the blast zone. It was time to find Llanzo Gayle.

9

"**D**ammit, Ren," I snapped as his phone went to voicemail for the third time. I glared at the phone as I ended the call. This wasn't good. Ren should have gotten back to me by now, especially given it was his daughter who was in trouble. It made me wonder why he hadn't. I'm sure he had a good reason, given the circumstances, but it was starting to piss me off because I actually needed his help since I had no idea how to find Llanzo Gayle, and after what had happened the last time I'd tried to get some information, I was hesitant to try again.

I glanced over my shoulder back toward La Cabana de Jamaica and frowned. I was still too close for comfort, but I didn't want to get too far away. If I left the city, I'd be hard pressed to find

Llanzo. And I had to find him soon. With each moment I spent standing around on the street, Ren's daughter became that much harder to find.

Maybe I'd been going about this all wrong. So far, I'd been going at this lone ranger style, and maybe what I needed was some help. Only, Max hadn't shown up yet. If he didn't get here soon, it might not matter that he was coming. Worse, I'd already wasted almost a day just getting here, and I had no illusions that anyone I called would be in a similar situation. I just couldn't wait that long.

It was time to get a move on, and that meant I had to think. It was hard because I didn't know the city at all. I glanced down at myself and sighed. I was dirty as hell and had blood spattered across me. Not enough for someone to notice what it was at first glance, but if I got stopped for any length of time, it'd be obvious.

First thing's first. Get some new clothes. I nodded, satisfied with a plan that didn't feel too difficult and looked around the small street. On the corner was a small shop practically dwarfed by the jerked chicken restaurant on its left. Even from here I could tell they sold clothing.

I glanced around, noted the cars speeding past and made a mad dash across the two-lane street. I hit the center divider just as a blue Civic sped by, missing me by inches. The driver threw a one-fingered salute in my direction, but I ignored him. I'd been the one jaywalking after all.

This time I took a few seconds to study the lane in front of me. The only car that could potentially hit me was way too far away to run me over. I sucked in a deep breath and sprinted across the remaining stretch of street.

I made my way across the sidewalk and stepped through the tropical bushes that divided the parking lot from the outside world. There weren't many cars in the parking lot of the place, and those that were had crowded toward the restaurant's side, making me think the store would be pretty empty.

Good. The last thing I wanted was for someone to get a good look at me.

I pushed open the heavy glass door and found myself staring at exactly one person. The clerk. The five-foot-nothing woman was curvy with tanned skin, but her nose was a little too crooked, and her teeth were a little too yellowed.

"Hello, looking for something in particular?" she said, voice slightly tinged with a Cuban accent as she turned to wave at me. She stopped, hand halfway into the air. "Why are you covered in blood?"

"Look, I've had a long day. I just want to get some clothes. I left mine at the hotel and don't have time to go back for them. Just help me out and there's an extra hundred bucks in it for you, personally," I replied, moving down toward the racks of shirts at the back of the store, and thanking my lucky stars it was empty.

She bit her lip, thinking for a moment before nodding. "Well, let me know when you're ready. We're a bit slow what with the commotion a few blocks away." She shivered. "Serves them right though. Those bastards are always killing each other. Makes it hard to make a living." As I turned to look back at her, she blushed and looked away, suddenly embarrassed by her words.

Part of me wanted to ask her more about it, but I didn't want to scare her before I got what I needed. There'd be plenty of time for that after I got changed.

I grabbed a black long-sleeve rashguard, a green and red Rastafarian-style Hawaiian shirt, a pair of khaki cargo shorts, and a pair of boxers with the Jamaican flag across the crotch. My strap-on sandals were okay, but I really just wanted some tennis shoes. Unfortunately, a quick look around left me wanting.

They'd have to do for now.

"Say, is there a changing room?" I asked, showing my bundle to the clerk. "I'd love to try these on."

"Unfortunately, no," she said, looking me over. "We do have a tiny bathroom. It's only for employees, but if you promise to buy, I could let you use it."

"Thanks, I'd appreciate it," I said, trying to smile at her, and she nodded once.

"Okay," she said, leaving her spot beside the register and moving toward a door a little ways away marked employees only. She unlocked it with a key and pulled it open to reveal a backroom stuffed to the gills with boxes. On the left side was a small door with a restroom placard.

"It's right through there," she said, indicating the door. "Don't be long because I can't really leave the store unattended to check on you."

"I'll be as quick as I can," I replied, nodding to her as I moved toward the bathroom in the back.

Once inside the restroom, I locked the door so no one would bother me while I changed even though there was only one other person in here.

Since there wasn't any good place to hang up my new clothes, and I was loath to put them on the floor of a public bathroom, I stuffed them on top of the faucet. Hopefully, they wouldn't fall in the sink. I turned on the hot water and much to my surprise, nothing came out.

"Swell," I muttered. They'd shut off the hot water, probably to save money. Cheap bastards.

Thankfully, the cold water did work. It splashed out of the faucet and struck the cheap ceramic bowl in a torrent. I quickly cleaned my hands, washing an insane amount of blood and grit down the sink. It was hard to believe the clerk hadn't just called the cops, even with the bribe.

As I stared at myself in the scratched mirror above the sink, I realized why she probably hadn't. I looked dirty sure, and while I knew it was blood and what not streaked across my face, shirt, and shorts, no one else would thanks to the dark colors.

It made me realize how much I'd been through since stepping off the plane and how much I still had to do. I needed to save Ren's daughter, and to do that, I had to find Llanzo Gayle. So far, it seemed like a nearly insurmountable task.

When I'd taken on the Scorpions, I'd at least had people to bounce ideas and strategies off of, had people who could help me. This was different, and nearly every move I'd made so far had nearly gotten me killed.

I had to be more careful because even with time counting down, I wouldn't do Ren's daughter any good if I got killed. No, I had to take things a bit slower, plan my attacks better, and ensure they'd succeed.

At the same time, I still had to move because she *didn't* have a lot of time, and I had no illusions that the cops would find them. The best case scenario for the cops was that they were being paid to stay out of the way.

No. It was up to me, and if Ren or Max called, then they could help, but as things stood, I had to move, had to get things done. And for Mary Ann, I could do just that.

I stripped off my clothes and flung them next to the pathetic black trashcan in the corner.

Once I was naked, I realized the rest of me wasn't much better what with the streaks of blood and the cuts, scratches, and bruises. My ribs were an ugly shade of yellowish purple, and as I touched them with my index finger, a stab of pain nearly made me cry out. That collision with the car had really done a number on me, and now that the adrenaline was starting to wear off, I realized how much I hurt. Only pain wouldn't help me. Finding Llanzo would.

I pushed the pain out of my mind and plunged my hands into the sink's freezing water to wash off the smears of blood. I scrubbed my flesh until the draining water ran clear. I let out a slow breath as cold water ran down the back of my neck and decided I needed to get myself a real shower with warm water if I wanted to get really clean. So far, I'd just assaulted the grime with cold water and soap so cheap it couldn't even get the gunk out from beneath my fingernails.

"I just need to get out of here and find Ren's daughter," I mumbled to myself before I pulled on my new underwear. "Then I can worry about showering. That's what's most important."

After I was dressed, I gathered up the remnants of my bloody clothing and dumped it in the trash instead of leaving it on the floor. That done, I moved toward the door, intent on letting myself out of the place.

I unlocked the door and stepped out into the shop to see two hulking men in tank tops beating the hell out of the clerk.

10

"What the hell do you think you're doing?" I yelled at the thugs beating up the five-foot-nothing brunette.

The two brutes glanced at me from across the laundromat with mud-colored eyes. The closer of the pair was the bigger of the two. His bulk seemed to overflow out of his sweat-stained white tank top, making me think of someone who had probably played sports in high school but had since let a few too many trips to the bar build up over his muscles. He turned his shaved head back toward the brunette, ignoring me.

"Stop." I took a step forward, my hands clenched as my eyes zeroed in on the woman's raven-colored hair still clutched in the thug's meaty fist. Blood dribbled from her split lips and down her chin, and her left eye was swollen shut.

The thug holding her raised his other hand to slap her.

"I said stop." I took another step forward as a red film of rage filled my vision.

"What have we here?" the smaller thug, a tattooed white gorilla with shaved head said. He raised one pierced eyebrow as he watched me cross the room. "Some kind of hero?" He cracked his massive neck. "Why don't you just sit your ass down? We'll be with you in a moment."

"I'm not a hero. I'm just a jarhead who is too dumb to know when to quit," I said as the idea of Mary Ann getting beaten up by her ex-boyfriend filled me. Rage and anger at the situation filled me to the brim. These guys weren't that jerk, but the look in their eyes was the same.

"Oh, a Marine? Think that makes you tough?" the bigger one asked. He smacked the tiny brunette causing her to yelp in pain. He tossed her across the cheap linoleum floor.

She bounced once and slid to a stop a few feet away. The urge to beat them into a bloody pulp so they'd know what it was like roared up inside me. My eyes snapped from the brunette on the floor to the musclebound, tatted-up skinhead coming toward me.

My right hand tightened into a fist as I took my own step forward. His mouth curled into a snarl as he reached out one hand toward me. I grabbed his wrist with my left hand and twisted while stepping in close. His wrist snapped in my grip as he came crashing down to the floor, forehead bouncing off the linoleum with a wet smack.

"I thought you guys were tough," I said, kicking the skinhead in the face. His nose shattered as he flopped onto his back, face a mask of scarlet.

The bigger guy stared back at me. Rage and horror spread across his face, and he snarled something intelligible. He lunged at me, crossing the ten feet between us in an instant. I slammed my right forearm into his throat. As his eyes bugged out of his head, I drove my foot into his knee, shattering it.

He crashed to the ground, gasping for breath as I reared back and kicked him again. My foot caught him under the chin, snapping his head backward. As his eyes rolled up in the back of his head, the sound of a gunshot obliterated my hearing. A bullet shattered the front window, spraying glass out across the sidewalk as I whirled around.

The thug with the broken wrist was holding a

gun in his shaking left hand. He pulled the trigger again, sending a shot into the wall beside me. I drew my Beretta in one swift motion and fired. The round obliterated his face as the gun he'd been holding flattered emptily to the floor.

Not wanting to take any chances, I searched the unconscious thug but found only fifty bucks in cash.

The woman was sitting up, watching me with a look on her face that was part relief and part fear. Did she think I was going to come after her next?

"Are you okay?" I asked, taking the thug's .40 Glock 23 and shoving it into my pocket. I moved toward her and offering her my hand.

"Yeah, thanks," she said, swallowing hard as she fixed her brown eyes on me.

"You should probably get out of here," I replied as I pulled her to her feet. "I'm not sure what was going on, but I'm willing to bet those aren't the type of guys who like getting beat up."

She nodded once and pulled her shaking hand away.

"You're right." She nodded once and took a deep breath before mumbling something in what sounded like Spanish. Then she turned her eyes back to me. "Those are Llanzo's boys. We need to get out of here before they recover." She shook her head. "Thanks for saving me, but I'm worried you might have made things worse. Llanzo will definitely trash the place when he finds out what happened."

"Wait, those are Llanzo's boys?" I asked. "You mean Llanzo Gayle, the crime lord?"

"Yes. They stopped by for protection money even though I'd already paid the Albanians," she said by way of an explanation.

"Do you know where I could find Llanzo?" I asked as she moved to the register and hitting a button that caused the drawer to spit out. She hastily gathered up the cash, shoving it in a green sack that had been in the drawer.

Satisfied, she stood, holding the bag to her chest and stared at me very hard. "Why do you want to know where Llanzo is?" The words came out of her mouth slowly, like she had weighed the question and wasn't sure if she really wanted to know the answer.

"You heard about the Jamaican Wave, right? The boat that disappeared. My friend's daughter was on it." I took a deep breath. "I'm going to get her back."

"I can't imagine what that's like," she replied as

she headed toward the door. "But there's nothing you can do."

"I've gotta try, miss." I let out a slow breath. "If not, I couldn't live with myself."

"Have you tried going to the police?" she asked, gesturing at the thugs. "Because what you're doing is a good way to get yourself killed."

"Not yet." I glanced back at the thugs. Neither of them were moving. Good. The last thing I wanted was for them to get up and force me to knock them out again. "I think that if they knew what to do, they'd have done it."

"I know I'm going to regret this," she whispered like she was talking to herself before meeting my eyes with her own. "But I know Llanzo has a club called the Montego Room. I've never gone there myself because my brother handles all of that stuff," she waved her hand anxiously, "But I could show you. It feels like the least I could do."

"That seems like it might put you in danger," I said as she turned headed toward the exit.

"Then don't come," she replied, steel in her voice. "It doesn't matter, really. After this, I'm already in danger. My best bet is they get madder at you than me. You seem like the kind of guy who could make Llanzo mad enough to forget about this."

She shoved open the door and disappeared through it without so much as a backward glance. That wouldn't do. I needed to find Llanzo, and while I could probably find the Montego Room, it would be easier if she just showed me.

I pushed through the door intent to take her up on her offer. She was only a few feet away. She glanced furtively up and down the street like a mouse searching for cats. When she spied me, her lips quirked into a tense smile.

"Do you need something, mister?" she asked while shoving the money bag into her purse.

"I've decided to accept your offer," I said, hoping I wouldn't be putting her in more danger. Only she was a grown woman, who knew the stakes better than me. She could make her own decisions.

"Okay," she said fear flashed through her eyes for a second. It made me feel like a jerk for accepting her offer, but now I couldn't go back on it.

"Thank you," I said, allowing my gratitude to flood into my voice. "I really appreciate it."

"You're welcome." She nodded, adjusting her

purse over her shoulder and held her hand out to me. "By the way. I'm Benita, and you are?"

"Billy," I said shaking her hand.

"Nice to meet you, Billy. Now let's go. I want to be back home before those guys wake up." Then she turned and began walking toward the bus stop down the block.

11

"You didn't have to pay for me," Benita's gaze remained fixed outside the window of the bus, watching as the cars passed us by.

"It was the polite thing to do," I said, shrugging. While the bus wasn't my first choice for transportation, it wasn't like I had other options since Benita didn't have a car and it was too far to walk.

"Realistically, the best thing for you to do would be to get off this bus right now. We're still a few stops away from the Montego Room, and once you go in, you may not come out." She glanced at me with worry filled eyes.

"I'm not getting off this bus until I see the Montego Room," I said. "That's just the way it is."

"I don't know you that well, Billy, but something

tells me you're as stubborn as a mule," she said, narrowing her eyes at me.

"I've heard that a time or two," I replied, glancing up toward the driver. She was a younger black woman with dreadlocks, and aside from her and the two of us, there were only a couple other people inside. Fortunately, they were all at the front of the bus while we were in the back so I didn't think anyone would hear us.

"So you say." She waved off my comment with one hand. The nubs of her nails had been bitten down so far, it was a wonder she wasn't bleeding. Without thinking, I snatched her hand before she could go back to gnawing on her fingers. Her eyes widened as I reached out and brushed a lock of hair from her face.

"Do those guys come around often? Llanzo's guys?" I said, my eyes roaming over her face. "Because if they do, maybe it's a good thing I'm going to see him."

"You can't fix things," she replied, color spreading across her cheeks. "You can just die trying. Many others have tried. Why would you be different?" She laughed. "You talk a good game, Billy, but at the end of the day, guys like Llanzo never stop."

"That's just because no one has hit him hard enough yet," I said, releasing her hand and looking past her out the window. Outside, a thin black woman trailed by a gaggle of kids was busy inspecting the meager produce at a fruit stand and putting the rare fruit or vegetable into a straw basket. One of her kids reached up to grab an apple, and she smacked his hand and admonished him. It made me wonder if they couldn't afford the fruit.

"What are you doing?" she asked in a voice so quiet, I almost didn't hear her. "You come here to save one girl, and now you want to save me too?"

"I just want to help where I can," I said, turning back to look at her. Everywhere people struggled to make ends meet, and I was willing to bet a huge portion of that was because of Llanzo.

"Is that so?" Her gaze moved from my face to my hands and back up to my face. The look in her brown eyes gave me the impression she'd seen things deep inside me.

"It is so." I nodded. "I may not do things the right way, but they're always for the right reasons."

"Even still, you shouldn't go after Llanzo," she whispered, and I had to strain to hear her speak. She bit her lip nervously but didn't look away from me. "It's not smart, and it's definitely not safe for either of us."

"Look, my friend needs help. You need help. Everyone needs help." I let out a slow breath. "I'm the help."

"You don't even know me," she replied, voice serious. She looked down at her hands and took a huge gulp of air.

"Maybe not, but that doesn't mean I can't help," I said, shrugging. "Either way, I'm going to try."

"Maybe," she replied, turning back toward the window to stare out at the street. "But I've been to this particular rodeo before, Billy. You have no idea what will happen once you go in there. Llanzo Gayle isn't a nice guy."

"Neither am I," I said as our bus rolled to a stop.

As the doors opened at our stop, she opened her mouth to say something, only before she did, her eyes went wide. In a flash, she'd shimmied down into the tiny space between the floor and the seat in front of us and pulled me down on top of her.

"Maybe they didn't see us——" she said before a single gunshot exploded through the tiny enclosed space, letting me know how very wrong she was.

"We know you're in here," the big guy I'd knocked out in Benita's shop said.

My heart sped up in my chest, crashing against my ribs as I heard his boots coming down the hallway.

"Damn," I muttered, pulling out the silenced Beretta.

"Billy, what are you doing?" Benita hissed as I leapt to my feet and pointed my gun at the thug.

He smiled at me and slowly raised his hands. "Well, if it isn't Mr. Marine," he said.

"Drop the gun," I said, and he complied, releasing his grip on his Glock and letting it hit the empty seat next to him.

"I'm going to enjoy pulling off each of your fingernails," he said right before something grabbed me around the throat, constricting my airflow. I was jerked backward off my feet and dragged with my legs trailing painfully. One hand went up to the noose around my neck, but before I could get a grip on it, my back smashed against something hard with a metallic clang that made me bite my tongue.

The iron tang of blood filled my mouth as I tried to suck in a breath. I tried to move, to pull myself free, but before I could move more than a few inches, someone kicked me in the ribs.

"I hear you like to play hero," rasped a low, hungry female voice in my ear. The hair on the back of my neck stood straight up. "I love breaking heroes."

"Who do we have in there?" I felt a tongue scrape along my cheek. "Right now, you're thinking this is the end, but it isn't. Not by a longshot." As darkness encroached on my vision, a flaming icepick of pain stabbed my brain.

No. It wasn't ending like this. As the noose around my neck cinched down tighter, I angled the gun in my hand behind me and pulled the trigger.

A scream filled my ears, and the noose loosened, allowing me to suck in a breath. I jerked my body forward, stumbling away from my attacker as the thug from earlier moved for his Glock.

I put two quick rounds in his chest, sending him flopping backward onto the seat in a bloody heap as people began to scream for real. I ignored it all, pushing down the distractions as I turned back toward the person who'd tried to strangle me.

My vision cleared enough for me to make out a tiny black girl with lavender eyes. Her blood-red lips were curled in an enraged grimace as blood oozed from a wound in her bicep. Her other hand held a gun that wasn't pointed at me—it was pointed at Benita.

"I expected more from the one who took down the Albanians," she said, holding up one purple-nailed hand and pointing her index finger at me. "Don't try to deny it either. I know it was you."

"Let her go," I said, glaring at her. "Now."

"And what if I don't?" she asked, raising an eyebrow at me.

"I'll shoot you in the face," I replied, hoping we weren't about to get swarmed by people. We were at a stop just a block away from where Benita had said the Montego Room would be, and I didn't doubt they'd brought reinforcements.

"I'd like to see you try it before I kill the girl," she replied, pain lacing her words.

"If you kill her, then I'll definitely shoot you." I narrowed my eyes. "Go ahead, do it. See what happens."

"Mmm," she purred, voice thick and husky as she stared at me through half-lidded eyes. "You've got the kind of eyes that make me think you'd actu-ally let me shoot her." She licked her lips as a slow grin spread across her face. "Interesting."

"Drop the gun, and I won't shoot you," I said,

glancing from her to Benita and back again. "I won't ask again."

"Honey, do you have any idea what I'm being paid to kill you?" She shook her head very slightly.

"You can't spend money if you're dead. I have my gun pointed at you. There's no way you don't die here. Your only plan is to drop it and hope I'm nice enough to let you live."

"That's what I'd planned to do." She bent down close to Benita and ran her fingers over the girl's cheek. "But think for a minute. What do you think happens to her?"

"Nothing because you're letting her go," I said.

"Maybe." She touched her chin with one long fingernail and looked into my eyes. "Don't get me wrong, normally by this time you'd already be dead, but you got lucky." She sucked on her fingertip once more and closed her eyes in near ecstasy. "Think on this though. I didn't come alone."

"Your friends aren't here yet. So what are you going to do?" I said. "You have one second to decide. Then I'm pulling this trigger."

"Is that so?" she asked totally serious.

"Yes." I narrowed my eyes, sighting my gun on her overly made-up face.

"Guess we're rolling the dice then." She pushed

her gun against Benita's temple. "Any last words?"

Benita opened her mouth like she was going to say something, but instead, threw herself to the side, trying to shift out of range of the gun. I fired as the assassin's barrel scraped along Benita's face. The assassin girl's finger started to depress the trigger as my shot caught her in the shoulder. Her own shot went wide, burying itself in the seat inches from Benita's head as the gun slipped from her hand and clattered to the floor.

"Come on," I said as the assassin slumped to the ground. I grabbed Benita by the hand, pulling her to the feet while I kicked the assassin's gun across the bus.

As Benita came to her feet, I saw the assassin girl dive through the back entrance to the bus. Damn. She began to run as I pulled us out of the bus. Then I turned to look at Benita.

"Go," I said as urgently as I could before releasing her and turning back toward the assassin.

The assassin girl was running away. Blood poured from her wounded shoulder, and I knew she wouldn't be using either arm very well for a while.

"Stop, or I'll shoot you," I called.

"And if I don't?" the girl called back at me in a bitchy tone. "What will you do? Shoot me?"

"Get down!" Benita cried, tackling me to the ground.

We crashed to the asphalt as a guy in a cowboy hat, blue jeans, and a white chamois button up stepped out of the car in front of the assassin girl and opened up on me with a stockless Uzi. The shots passed so close to me the wind from them stung my eyes. His gun bucked like a bronco in his hands as I fired at him with my Beretta. The shots caught him in the face, blowing out his life. His Uzi clattered to the floor as I leapt to my feet.

I tackled the assassin just as she was reaching for the fallen Uzi. The front of her head cracked against the street, and her eyes went glassy and far off. The weapon went skittering across the street, and I pointed my Beretta at the still stunned assassin.

"Don't shoot her," Benita pleaded.

"Why?" I asked, confused, but instead of responding to my question, she pointed behind me.

"Because we need to get out of here!" she cried.

I turned my head to see the strobing lights of police cars coming straight toward us. I wasn't quite sure why they were here already, or who had called them, but it didn't matter. She was right. We needed to get out of here, right now.

12

"We'll meet again!" the assassin called from behind me as Benita and I raced away from her. The voice in my head had told me to shoot her, but there was a huge difference between being spotted from far away with what might or might not be a pistol in your hand and shooting someone in plain view of the police.

That didn't make it feel like the smart play, though. If Iraq had taught me anything, it was that second chances to put people down cost a lot more than first chances did.

"We need to find somewhere to lie low," I huffed at Benita. "If we do, I can get us out of here, okay?"

"Okay," she said between gulps of air. "There's a parking garage not too far from here. Maybe we can go there?"

As I rounded the corner, I shoved my Beretta into the pocket of my cargo pants so it wouldn't be immediately visible to the gaggle of patrons surrounding a local souvenir seller.

"Sounds like a plan," I replied as the sound of a helicopter in the distance filled my ears. "Damn."

"What?" she asked, glancing at me before looking over her shoulder for a gunman. "I don't see anyone."

"Sounds like a helicopter, but it's too far away for me to be sure." I looked around for something to help us get away. A guy on a crotch rocket motorcycle was coming down the road. As he slowed to weave around some cars, I stepped out into the street and clotheslined him right off his bike. The move made me feel bad even though he wasn't going fast enough to get seriously hurt because traffic was at a near standstill.

The rider crashed to the ground flat on his back, his black and white helmet smacking into the asphalt with a sickening thud. I paused just long enough to lift the green Yamaha FZ-09 off the street and spin it around so it was facing oncoming financially and spiritually by these toxic types. They have been battered in every way imaginable and as you read in the beginning of this book, some of them were pushed over the edge—the victims of a silent crime where the perpetrators will rarely be held accountable for their actions or were only held accountable when it was far too late.

Survivors often feel so alienated by this form of covert abuse that they feel they have nowhere to turn. Mental health professionals and advocates alike are gradually beginning to expose psychological violence, but not at a rate where every single therapist is familiar with these dynamics. I would caution any marriage or couple's therapists to be wary of these types, as they can manipulate therapists very well into thinking the victim is the abuser. Friends and family members may be the abusers themselves or they may easily invalidate the experiences of survivors because until they have experienced it themselves, they will struggle to understand exactly what is taking place. I have heard too many tales where the criminal justice system, the friends and family members of victims and the harem members of the malignant narcissist take the side of the abuser over the victim—all because of their false mask.

Remember that before you read about narcissistic abuse, you were prone to excusing your abuser's actions, denying them, minimizing them or rationalizing them. As a survivor of abuse, you may have also blamed yourself for "provoking" your abuser somehow because that is what the abuser wanted you to believe. It's difficult to explain that this is not a normal relationship or even your run-of-the-mill dysfunctional one because usually, the latter takes two dysfunctional people who don't know how to communicate in a healthy manner. In fact, while told the full truth of what you were experiencing to anyone, fearing that they would not believe you.

The harsh truth is, they may not believe you, unfortunately, and that has to do with the way we stigmatize abuse survivors in society, making them feel ashamed about the fact that they were abused in the first place. Many victims attempt to "play up" the romantic moments with their abusers to others, or emphasize everything that is going well, as a coping mechanism—it enables them to pretend that everything is fine, when in fact, behind closed doors, the victim is fighting for survival each and every day of his or her life. This is probably why it is so easy for the narcissist is swoop in and work his or her magic, telling everyone who will listen that the victim is "unhinged" and that the narcissistic abuser did "so much" for them, while the victim stayed silent about the transgressions that went on for years.

In an abusive relationship, the dysfunction lies primarily within the behavioral patterns of the abuser, though the effects of trauma can certainly cause the victim to engage in maladaptive coping mechanisms and lash out in ways uncharacteristic of them. The victim may attempt to cope with the trauma in various ways, trying to take back their power by sometimes even resorting to using the same tactics that a narcissist uses, but failing to engage in them as heartlessly. As a result, they feel more and more ashamed and the abuser then uses their behavior as justification for the abuse, even while knowing very well that had the victim never been abused in the first place for such a long period of time, they would not have reacted in such a way.

This does not make the dynamic "mutual abuse," just

spect. We must remember that the survivor has become locked into a traumatized state and then becomes increasingly triggered by the narcissist. They may then resort to certain maladaptive coping mechanisms to survive. The survivor of this type of abuse then needs to take agency to find healthier ways of coping, but that does not make the victim the abuser (even though the abuser will certainly try to convince them they are). The victim goes into the relationship with the intention of loving and caring for someone in a reciprocal relationship; the abuser goes into the relationship as a scam artist, as someone who controls, manipulates and erodes the victim's reality slowly but surely, exploiting the victim for all they are worth. There is a power imbalance as the victim tries to over-communicate and express his or her feelings to their abuser to no avail, attempting to express how much the abuser has hurt them while the abuser "hoovers" the victim back in with pity ploys, fake displays of remorse or shallow apologies that never incorporate changes in behavior or empathy for the victim.

The bottom line is: garden-variety emotionally unavailable people, Complex PTSD and trauma survivors and victims of narcissists are capable of evolution. They're capable of high degrees of empathy, of remorse. They not only know right from wrong, they often discern between it when it comes to their behavior. Malignant narcissists? They couldn't care less about who they hurt in the process. Each and every one of us has probably engaged in a toxic behavior or two in our lifetime—that doesn't mean we engage in a chronic pattern of abuse or that we are abusers or toxic narcissists. We are simply human—but we never deserve to be abused.

If you want to know if you're in trouble, ask yourself: am I

ually or otherwise abused? If the answer is yes, the problem goes beyond just incompatibility or emotional unavailability. Whether a person is a true malignant narcissist or not becomes less important than their chronic pattern of behavior—their long-term behavior will tell you everything you need to know, even when labels seem to fail.

traffic before jumping on. The whole thing had taken less than half a second.

"Get on!" I called, gesturing at Benita with one hand.

She did as she was told. As she wrapped her arms around my waist, I gunned the bike, weaving through the stopped traffic as quickly as I could. Even with the Yamaha racing through the streets, the sound of the helicopter getting closer filled my ears. I hazarded a glance over my shoulder and saw it cutting through the sky like a bird of prey.

It wasn't a police helicopter. It was all black and had a guy hanging out the side with what looked like belt-fed Browning M2 machinegun capable of firing over four hundred fifty rounds of .50 BMG in about a minute.

"I'm starting to wish you'd just let me get beat up," Benita replied, gripping me tighter and burying her face against my back as I bore down on the bike. The engine roared, pushing us forward, but thanks to all the traffic, it wasn't enough. The helicopter was gaining on us.

Assuming they wanted to shoot up a street, the helicopter's Browning M2 would have us in range long before we got away.

"Where's that parking garage—" The rest of

my words were cut off as gunfire erupted from the helicopter. Round after round tore up the street just behind us.

"Make a left!" Benita screamed in my ear.

I twisted the bike sideways as I executed the turn and found myself staring at a parking garage. Cover! Thank God.

Bullets ripped into the cement pillars supporting the parking structure as we zoomed inside. Only before we made it even a few feet, I realized we were in trouble. The entrance gate was down. Before we could crash into it, I skidded to a stop and slammed my hand onto the button beside the entrance. As the gate came up, I gunned the bike. Our tires spun, catching the cement in a screech of burning rubber.

"Well, this is fun. I can't wait for our second date," Benita said, a touch of humor in her voice as we rocketed forward into the depths of the garage.

"So what's the plan?" I asked, ignoring her comment about the date as I looked around to see if anyone had followed inside. No one had so far, but if these guys were willing to shoot at us in broad daylight, I was willing to bet they'd be on us soon.

"We find another vehicle and leave out the exit

before they come inside and kill us?" she offered, and to be fair, it wasn't a bad plan.

Part of me worried they might just shoot every car that left, but something made me doubt they'd do that. It hadn't seemed like they'd actually hit anyone when they'd shot at us. Besides, it wasn't like I had a better plan.

We rode toward the exit as the sound of the helicopter's thumping blades along with police sirens filled the air. Before we reached it, I pulled to a stop beside an old VW Bus. It'd definitely seen better days, but that was fine because it was just going to be cover for now.

Taking a deep breath, I kicked the stand on the bike into place and hopped off, heading toward it.

"What are you doing?" Benita asked as I tried the doors and found them locked. Too bad.

"Getting us a new ride." I smashed my Beretta into the driver's window, shattering it into bits of gummy glass. I swept the frame with the weapon before reaching in and unlocking it.

"Are you stealing a car?" she asked as I swept the glass off the seat and got in. Then I reached across the van to the passenger side and unlocked it.

"Yes. Get in," I said, moving to hotwire the car. It roared to life as she slid in the passenger seat.

"At least you know what you're about," she said, as I put my foot on the gas and moved forward into the corridor. No one had come in yet, but that didn't mean they wouldn't. As I headed for the exit, the sound of the helicopter started to fade, which was probably because the police sirens were getting louder.

I reached the exit a moment later, and as I slid my ticket into the machine, it beeped and opened. Guess I hadn't been here long enough.

"Where are we going?" Benita asked as I pulled into the street and turned away from the sound of the sirens. "The Montego Room is back that way." She spun in her seat and pointed behind us.

"I'm going to go a few blocks away and drop you off. I'm not sure where you can go, exactly, but anywhere is safer than with me." My hands tightened on the steering wheel as I turned left onto a street and made my way through traffic.

"I think you might be right," she said, nodding at me. "Turn right up ahead."

"Okay." The rest of the drive passed in silence save for the directions she gave me, and before long she directed me to stop beside an old apartment building.

"This is my cousin's place. I doubt they'll come to look for me here just yet." She shot me a sad smile. "You really messed everything up, Billy." She leaned in and kissed me on the cheek before exiting the vehicle. "Let's hope you can fix it."

13

I wound up ditching the bus a few blocks away, ditching my shirt in exchange for a white T-shirt with a Red Stripe beer emblazoned across the chest, and a red baseball cap with the Jamaican flag on it.

Despite the streets being jammed with cops, the walk to the Montego Room was uneventful. As I stared at the bar's entrance, I could hear dance music raging inside. Palm trees surrounded the parking lot, making it feel enclosed and cut off from the outside world, and as I glanced around, I was surprised to see the lot nearly filled to the brim. Even relatively early in the afternoon, the place was filled with patrons. Part of me was happy about that. It'd make it a lot easier to sneak inside unnoticed.

The building itself reminded me of those modern dance clubs you see in movies about Las Vegas. The walls were floor to ceiling frosted glass with images of Jamaican street art emblazoned on it in golds and silvers. The name Montego Room blazed with neon light at the top next to a pair of blazing torches. More torches lined the sidewalk along the building, giving off the scent of citronella as they burned. Red velvet ropes were strung between the torches to rein in the line that was practically around the building.

A burly bouncer in a shirt two sizes too small for him. He sat outside the bar's entrance, and as I watched him pat each and every person down, I was immediately glad I'd ditched my weapons. Judging by his quick, methodical movements, he'd have found my gear in a second.

Plastering a drunk tourist grin on my face, I moved to back of the line. It moved along quickly to let me know the holdup was from the security and not because they were arbitrarily keeping people outside, and after about ten minutes, I'd gotten to the front of the line.

The bouncer stared at me with flat, black eyes as he stood in front of his wooden three-legged stool. He took a step forward, one hand on his hip, the other outstretched toward me. He waited like that, body hulking beneath his black tank top and camouflage pants for about three seconds while he looked me up and down.

"ID?" he asked, curling his sausage fingers back and forth.

"Sure thing," I said, pulling my ID out of my wallet and offering it to him.

He glanced at it for half a second before nodding.

"I'm going to frisk you now. Don't make any sudden movements," he said, gesturing for me to put my ID away.

"Okay," I said, no sooner had the word left my mouth then he was running his hands over my body in quick, professional movements. Satisfied, he nodded and sat down on his stool.

"Go on in," he said, gesturing toward the door before turning his attention to the honeymooners behind me.

"Thanks," I replied, shoving my wallet back in my pocket before stepping through the green and red painted wooden doors.

It was so loud inside I could barely think. The crushing beat of reggae music mixed with strobe lights nearly gave me a headache as I pushed through the massive crowd and moved toward the back. The air tasted like body odor and vomit with just the faintest hint of marijuana over the top of it, but as I got closer to the dark curtained area in the back, the smell of weed got stronger and stronger.

The walls themselves were filled with Rastafarian print, and the floor beneath my feet was checkered red and green tile. Framed pictures of Bob Marley filled the walls, and as I surveyed the place, I saw that the bars all were done in sleek metal and glass. People bustled about the small tables in front of the bars while still more gyrated on the dance floor.

After glancing around one last time just to make sure no one was following me, I sucked in one last breath and pushed myself past the rest of the patrons toward the curtained area in the back. This was where Benita had said Llanzo's men would be.

Only, as I approached the curtain, a thin black man with bright pink hair looked up at me and puckered his lips like he'd bitten into something sour.

"Do you need something?" he asked, voice bored and uncaring.

"I'm looking for a little chemical enhancement,

if you know what I mean?" I replied, holding up a pair of hundreds.

"Sorry, we don't have anything like that here. We're a legal establishment." He shook his head.

I moved forward and pressed one of the bills into his hand. "Are you sure? I was told this was the place to fulfill all my needs." The man looked down at the bill in his hand and sighed.

"Look, buddy. I appreciate the gesture, but I can't help you," he whispered, handing me the bill back.

"Worth a try," I said, shrugging at him as I took the bill and pocketed it.

"I suppose—" I jabbed him in the throat with the knife edge of my palm. His eyes practically bugged out of his skull as he collapsed onto his knees in front of me. One hard knee to the chin sent him sprawling backward onto the concrete floor. I moved past him and stepped through the curtain.

A man with a shaved head and a nose ring looked up at me. "Who the hell are you?" he asked before looking at the blonde with her face buried in his lap. All I could see of her was the top of her head because the table concealed everything else. The confusion on the skinhead's face grew as he turned back to me, one big hand on the back of the girl's head.

"Whoever you are, you need to get out," he said, his voice only slightly slurred as he closed his eyes and leaned back against the red-cushioned wall. "And tell that asshat outside to get me a drink."

"Sure thing. Sorry for the trouble," I said, grabbing the rum bottle off the table between us.

I smashed the bottle into his face.

He shrieked, his nose exploding in a fountain of red goo as his eyes shot open. He reached up to grab his ruined face, and I hit him again as the blonde finally looked up, eyes glassy and unseeing. I ignored her.

"Who is the guy in charge of your little operation?" I grabbed the skinhead by the back of the head and slammed his face onto the table. Twice. "And where can I find him?"

"I'll take you to him," said a voice behind me just before I felt the cold kiss of a barrel press against the back of my head.

"I didn't even see you," I said and wasn't sure if the guy knew how much of a compliment it was. I hadn't seen anyone in here aside from the girl and the skinhead.

"Yeah, I hear that a lot," he said, and his voice was strangely familiar. I'd definitely heard it before but couldn't place it. "I can see your muscles tensing, so I'm pretty sure you're about to move. I wouldn't. You should just sit there and behave because I'll pull this trigger the second you so much as twitch. Now drop the rum bottle."

"Okay," I said, letting go of the rum bottle. It hit the table, causing it to wobble slightly before the bottle rolled off and shattered on the concrete floor.

"Good, now slowly put your hands up and—" I dropped, letting my full weight slam into the edge of the flimsy table.

Glasses and bottles hit the floor with a crash as I rolled under the table's falling edge and used it to shield myself.

A bullet splintered the wood next to my face as I grabbed the broken rum bottle. I came up swinging, my broken bottle cutting an arc through the air as the man danced backward out of reach.

My bottle passed harmlessly by him as he brought his gun around toward him. His features were hidden behind a black ski mask, but his eyes had the cold, dead look of a hired killer.

I threw the bottle at him while leaping over the table. The broken bottle caught him in the meaty part of his forearm because he'd swept his arm up to knock it away. Blood poured from the wound in his arm as he brought his arm back around to shoot me.

He fired a quick shot that ricocheted off the floor beside me as I launched myself into the air. My shoulder crashed into him, knocking him backward a few steps. As he stumbled, I hit the ground hard on my left hand while grabbing the broken neck of the bottle with my right. I sprang to my feet, bringing the broken glass upward in an arc that tore across his stomach in a bloody streak.

Blood gushed from the wound as he tried to bring his gun around, but I was too close for that. I drove my elbow into his neck, buckling him forward before slamming my knee into his face. His nose shattered as his head whipped backward, and he slumped to the floor unconscious.

I snatched up his gun and whirled around to point it at the skinhead who was still sitting there too stoned and too shocked to do much of anything. Hell, he hadn't even pulled up his pants.

Thankful the club was too loud for anyone to have heard the scuffle, I pressed the still hot barrel of the assassin's gun into his crotch. He yowled, but a quick glance over my shoulder let me know no one had come through the curtains yet.

"Tell me where to find Llanzo, or I swear you'll regret it," I snarled.

The skinhead swallowed so hard he nearly choked on his own spit as he lifted a trembling hand and pointed one shaking finger toward the left wall. A full-length painting of Bob Marley with a joint in one hand and his other arm at his side stood looking at us.

"That's just a painting," I said, backhanding the skinhead with the gun. His head snapped sideways, and blood spurted from his smashed lips. "Do you think I'm messing around?"

"There's a door just behind it," he squeaked, his words flecking blood on my new shirt. I turned to examine it again. I couldn't be sure if he was telling the truth.

"Guess we'll find out," I said, hauling the skinhead to his feet.

"What are you doing, man?" he asked right before I flung him into the portrait.

He crashed through the canvas, arms flailing as he tumbled through.

"Guess he wasn't lying," I mumbled, turning to

regard the blonde who had lain on the couch and closed her eyes.

As I moved to follow the skinhead into the hidden passageway, the assassin I'd knocked out groaned. I stared at him for a moment before putting a round in his heart. Couldn't risk him coming after me and shooting me in the back.

I made my way over to the skinhead and jerked him to his feet by the hoop in his ear. He whimpered, blood dripping down his face and staining his Metallica t-shirt.

"Let's go," I muttered, pushing him down the dimly lit corridor. "I'm in a hurry, and if you slow me down, I'll just shoot you."

The man nodded and stumbled forward, one hand on the wall for support. After only a few feet, we reached a bend, and as we rounded it, I found myself staring at a solid steel door set into a concrete wall.

A keypad that reminded me of a telephone was embedded above the handle in the door and seeing it made me glad I hadn't shot the thug.

"Open the door," I growled, shoving the skinhead toward the door.

"S-sure." The skinhead punched in his code, and the door unlocked with a sound that made me think it had electromagnetic locks. "See, no problem."

The skinhead seized the handle with one hand and jerked the door open. Gunfire exploded from the corridor beyond. Bullets tore into him, pitching him backward in a spray of blood and bone.

14

I threw myself behind the metal door as bullets slammed into it, pinging off the steel and ricocheting off the corridor. I crouched down, trying to control my breathing as my heart hammered in my chest.

Silence descended over the hallway, and as it did, I heard the sounds of boots scraping on concrete. Someone was coming to investigate. I crept backward a couple steps, to give me a good angle of the doorway while not revealing my position and lay on my stomach, stolen pistol aimed at the entrance.

Sure enough a few moments later a guy dressed in a black tank top and cargo pants came through the doorway. He had an AK-47 in his hands, and as he moved to sweep the room, I put a bullet in the side of his head. His life disappeared in a burst of brain and skull, and as he pitched sideways, I braced myself for return fire. Only none came.

As the echoes of my gunshot reverberated in my ears and the dead man slumped to the ground, I let out a slow breath and waited.

When a ten count passed with no more sounds from the corridor beyond, I unslung my phone, flipped it to the camera, and used it to look past the edge. It revealed no one in the dimly lit hallway. Had there just been the one guard?

I wasn't sure, but something had definitely gone wrong because the moment that door had opened, there'd been gunfire. Had the skinhead put in a code to let the guy on the other side know there was trouble?

If so, it'd been clever, but deadly for him. Either way, I was done wasting time here. Getting to my feet, I moved forward, pocketing my pistol and scooping up the AK-47. Then I searched the guy and found a Becker BK2 knife, and a grenade.

"What the hell do you need a grenade for down here?" I mused, putting the grenade into my pocket and strapping the knife sheath to my belt.

The small corridor beyond the door looked like it had been dug out of the earth with little more than framing in place afterward. Was it used just for ferrying stuff from the club and back and was therefore mostly unguarded?

That could definitely be the case if no one but the people who were supposed to be here were down here. Still, I didn't like it. Something about the setup smelled fishy.

Not that it mattered because I had to hurry and find Annabeth. This was my only lead, and if I didn't step on it, I might not find her at all. I took a deep breath, steeling myself before moving through the dark tunnel while doing my best to keep to the shadows.

After only a few meters, I came to a fork in the road. Both paths ended in a chain-link fence with a padlocked gate, and as I squinted to try to see past, it was no use because privacy slats had been slid through the links.

"When in doubt, go left, I guess," I mumbled to myself as I approached the gate. Only, as I did, I found that while the padlock had been slipped through the hasp, it hadn't actually been shut. I pulled it off the hasp and pushed the door open a couple inches to peer inside.

There was no one beyond the fence. I slipped behind the gate and pulled it shut after me. Then I followed the corridor for another few twisting meters before coming into a large room. Doorways lined the walls, but a quick glance into the first one let me know it was empty.

"I wonder if it's some kind of storage room?" I mused, checking the next one. They were all the same, about ten square feet with dirt walls and a dirt floor. There was a hook on the top where it looked like a battery-powered light could be hung, but none were in place.

It didn't take long to search the rooms, and as I approached the last room in the far left corner, I was about to give up and go back. Clearly, this path led to a dead end. Still, I'd come this far, so I might as well check.

I moved to the last room and peered inside to find it was different from the others. This one had a concrete floor and a stairwell that descended into the depths of the earth.

"Guess it wouldn't be the lair of a drug kingpin if it didn't have a subterranean hideaway," I grumbled, moving to the stairwell and peering down. It was lit with fluorescent lights that caused the grated, stainless steel stairs to feel cold and unfeeling.

Gun at the ready, I moved downward. The air

grew colder and colder as I went, but other than that, it was a fairly uneventful trip to the bottom

I soon found myself staring into a tiny room with a steel door like the one up top on one side and a battered steel desk along one wall. A man dressed similarly to the guard above sat in a metal folding chair with his feet propped up on the desk.

He was way too busy "reading" a magazine that was mostly pictures of half-naked women to notice me. He dabbed the ash from a cigarette into a white porcelain ashtray and moved it to his mouth, taking a long, slow drag. As he blew the smoke out, it drifted toward a grate overhead with a whirring metal fan.

Taking a deep breath, I stepped out into the room and pointed my AK-47 at him.

"Don't make a sound, or I'll kill you. Nod if you understand," I said, gesturing at him with the gun.

The man's eyes went wide as he looked up from me. The magazine slipped from his hands and hit the ground. He nodded and put his hands in his lap, clamping his fingers on his thighs.

"I want to find Llanzo Gayle," I said, taking a step closer. "Where is he?"

"Probably in his harem in the other wing. He doesn't usually come to the production floor. He has people for that." The man gulped. The sound of it echoed in the tiny room. "If you'd wanted to find him, you should have taken the other door." He nodded up at the ceiling.

"What's in there?" I asked, pointing at the metal door the man had been guarding.

"That's where we refine the drugs," he replied, and the smugness in his voice annoyed me.

"Are you lying to me?" I asked, narrowing my eyes at him.

"I thought about lying to you but decided it would be pointless. You'll just shoot me and check for yourself, anyway. This way, maybe you won't shoot me." He let out a slow breath. "If you go inside, you'll find a state of the art chemical facility capable of producing an endless supply of drugs."

"And Llanzo is upstairs?" I asked, thinking over what he'd said. It made sense, and the guy didn't seem to be lying.

"Yes. Well, maybe." He let out a sigh. "He may not be there, but if he was here, that's where he'd be."

"Okay." I took a step forward. "What's your code for the door?"

"Four, six, twelve," he replied, and I nodded.

"Thanks." I stepped forward and slammed the

butt of my weapon into his temple, knocking him unconscious, and he fell off his chair, sprawling onto the floor.

I took a step back and ran a hand through my hair as I stared at the door. While I wanted to check for sure, I was worried that if I went inside and it wasn't Llanzo's place, I'd just find myself facing down more security.

No. It'd be better to go check the other corridor. Something told me he wasn't lying, and besides, I was willing to bet Llanzo would have much better security. I turned back to the stairs and hurried up them two and three at a time.

As I stepped out of the stairwell and into the giant storage room at the top, I spotted a man at the far end of the room. He had his back to me, and was reasonably far away, but even still I could tell he was huge. Even beneath his forest green tank top, his huge back had so much muscle, it made me feel small in comparison.

While his size concerned me, a bullet would stop a musclebound giant just as well as anyone else. Just one problem. There was the masked group of soldiers standing just beyond him.

None of them had noticed me yet, since their faces were hidden beneath what looked like motorcycle helmets. Each had an AK-47 slung over their shoulder and hanging at their waist.

Edging back down out of sight, I pulled out the grenade I'd gotten from the guard at the entrance, flipped the spoon off the top, and sent it flying into the room. It clanged against the floor as I dropped back down the stairs. An explosion shook the room as I dropped down on my stomach, angling my AK toward the doorway as best I could without exposing myself.

I counted to ten, then to twenty, and when no one came through the doorway, I crawled forward, gun at the ready. Pieces of soldiers littered the blown-out room as a smoky cloud rose up from the center of the room, obscuring most of the carnage. I crept forward ready to put a hole in anything that moved.

Something smashed into the side of my head, sending the world into a tailspin. My vision went blurry as I stumbled sideways. My AK slipped from my fingers as the huge guy from earlier sprang out of the small storage room he'd been hiding in.

He swung a metal baton at me as he rushed me. His blow slammed into my stomach, making me buckle over as breath whooshed from my lungs. The strap of my AK slipped off my shoulder and hit the ground. His meaty paws wrapped around my face and slammed me backward into the wall.

My vision shattered into pinpricks of light as he wrapped his fingers around the waist of my pants and flung me bodily across the room.

I crashed into the floor a few feet away. Agony exploded through my body as the man grabbed me by the hair and hauled me to my feet.

I tried to grab onto his wrist, but he twisted his hand, jerking my head to the side. White-hot agony raged across my scalp, and I gritted my teeth, trying to ignore it, to throw it behind a mental wall honed by years of training in the corps.

It worked, but barely, and as he reared back to strike me, I kicked him. My foot caught him in the solar plexus as his other hand closed around my throat. The blow did little more than make him wobble, and he slammed me backward into the wall.

My vision went blurry as he pinned me against the wall with his forearm. I tried to suck in a breath, but it wouldn't come. I shut my eyes, forcing my body to move. My hand went into my pocket, and I pulled out the pistol I'd taken from the assassin.

The weapon in hand, I pulled it out and fired into his stomach. He stumbled backward, releasing me as his hands went to his own wounds. I collapsed to my knees, gasping for breath. Tears stung my eyes as I raised the gun and fired again.

The shot took him in the bridge of the nose, turning his life into a distant memory as he hit the ground. I sat there for another moment and wiped my eyes with the back of one hand. Each breath hurt like rusty razor-wire, but I knew I had to get up.

I moved forward, shoving the pistol back in my pocket as I scooped up one of the fallen AK-47s and eyed the exit. Part of me wanted to rush toward it, but instead, I moved through the room, looking for other survivors but found none.

Satisfied, I wiped the sweat from my brow with the back of one hand before making my way back through the corridor to the gate. There was no one there, and as I pushed the gate open, I looked for more guards. Only I didn't see anyone.

Part of me was surprised, after all, I'd used a grenade in that underground room. Then again, it was subterranean, and maybe the sound had been dampened too much?

I pushed the thought away and moved silently toward the other fork gate while keeping on the lookout for guards. Finding none, I checked the lock, but this one was, in fact, locked.

"Damn," I muttered as I put the AK to the padlock and let loose a short blast. The lock blew apart, and I waited a few seconds for my hearing to return, while I crouched down.

When no one came, I pushed the gate open.

15

I stepped through the gate and followed the corridor along until I found myself in another huge chamber. Unlike the last one, though, this one was well lit and filled with motorcycles, Humvees, and various other vehicles.

As I moved forward, approaching the edge of the cement walkway leading from the entrance to the carpark, I saw that asphalt covered the chamber's floor. That, combined with all the vehicles, made me think I was in some kind of underground vehicle bunker. Wasn't this where Llanzo was supposed to be? Had the guard below lied and made me backtrack all the way out to a parking lot?

While it seemed likely given the spread of vehicles before me, I didn't think the guard had lied, not with a gun to his head. While I wasn't a hundred percent certain of his innate truthfulness, I decided to search the bunker before heading all the way back down to the sealed door below.

Even still, as I surveyed the vehicles, I was angry at myself. I should have just checked out that door while I was down there. If I was forced to go back, I'd lose a lot of time, which was the one thing I didn't have enough of. Hell, if I'd just opened the door, maybe I'd have walked in on Llanzo and been on my way to Annabeth right now.

Of course, it was equally possible that would have just been another delay, one that would have taken enough time for Ren's daughter to be killed. I shook that thought away. Going over what could have been wouldn't help me now.

I dropped into a crouch and made my way forward. I scanned the walls of the bunker for other entrances but found none along the cement catwalk where I stood. It was possible there was a secret passage or something, but I couldn't find one right now.

As I turned back toward the vehicles gathered below and headed toward the stairs that led down to the garage floor, the Jeep directly below me exploded. A burst of gunfire chewed into the wall above the cement railing as I hit the ground. As something glinted to my right, I scrambled to my feet. I fired a short burst from my AK-47 at the glimmer just before the wall behind me exploded.

A wave of heat washed over me moments before the shockwave threw me off the embankment. My knees slammed into the cement with a staccato crack that made agony course through the lower part of my body as I crashed to the ground beside the flaming wreckage of the Jeep.

More gunfire ripped into the Jeep, puncturing the flaming metal and zinging by me as I lay there trying to remember how to breathe. My legs hurt so badly, I could barely move past it, but as the staccato bursts of bullets got closer and closer, I forced myself to move, to function.

I scrambled behind a white passenger van that looked suspiciously like the one that had blocked my escape outside the hotel and dropped to my belly. As I looked through the narrow gap between the ground and the van for the source of the attacks, I sucked in a breath and tried to calm down.

Across the garage was a large armored van with what looked like an M2 machinegun mounted to one side. A gunner wearing military fatigues and a green bandana sat behind the gun while another guy frantically moved to slide a new belt into place.

As they finished reloading, I sprang to my feet. My dive carried me past the edge of the van just before bullets damned near tore it in half. The smell of gasoline filled my ears an instant before it exploded, throwing me skidding across the pavement. The skin on my arms was torn to ribbons as I rolled ass over teakettle before coming to a stop behind a green, military-style Humvee.

As I lay there, stars spinning past my vision, the gunfire cut off. No doubt the gunner was looking for me. I got woozily to my hands and knees and wiped the blood from my eyes. The sound of boots on the ground filled my ears, and as I turned toward the sound, I saw the guy who had been loading the belt, coming toward the area.

I dropped back to my belly, lined up my own AK-47 on the guy and pulled the trigger. The blast caught him in the chest, flinging him backward. The M2 came to life then, whipping around and blasting the Humvee. Bullets pinged off its armored flesh as I huddled there behind the wheel-well.

As the world fell into sudden silence, I crept to the door of the Humvee and pulled the door open. More gunfire erupted from the M2, slamming into the vehicle and rocking it to the side as I climbed inside. As the windows shattered, spraying gummy bits of glass down on me, I rolled onto my back and stared at the passenger mirror. It revealed the shooter well enough for me to spray a few bullets in his general direction.

He ducked out of the way, diving back into his armored vehicle. I sprang from the Humvee, unloading my AK in quick bursts as I raced toward the guy. As my gun clicked empty, the soldier poked his head out, a Glock in hand. His first shot went wide as I drew my own pistol and fired back. While I didn't hit him, my shot was distracting enough for him to miss me again.

I fired again, causing him to duck for cover. I flung myself forward, rolling past the edge of the gun, and as I came up on my feet, he ducked out to shoot at me again. My finger squeezed the trigger as his gun came around, and my round caught him in the throat. Blood sprayed from the wound as he kept bringing around his own weapon.

Only before he could pull the trigger, I emptied my gun into him. He flopped backward into the vehicle as I moved forward, dropping my spent pistol and relieving him of his Glock.

As I looked around, scanning the cavern for

more enemies, the sound of helicopter blades filled my ears. I spun to see two camouflage-clad men helping a humungous FAT man in a white suit with a pink shirt into the same black helicopter that had shot at me just a few blocks away.

That was all the time I had before another contingent of soldiers surged from a door at the far end. I emptied the Glock at them, causing them to scramble for cover. As they tried to fire back while ducking away, I grabbed hold of the Browning M2 and let her rip. The rest of the bullets shot out across the enclosed space, turning the garage into a meat grinder that tore the soldiers to bits.

As the Browning spit the last of its rounds in their direction, those that had managed to find cover opened fire. I threw myself into the armored vehicle as the garage filled with lead death. Bullets ricocheted off the metal as I clambered into the front of the vehicle and slid behind the wheel. With bullets bouncing off the still-running armored van, I jerked it into gear and slammed my foot down on the gas.

The vehicle lurched forward toward the soldiers, bullets pinging off the metal shell and finally shattering the windshield. Safety glass rained down on me as smoke started to pour from under the hood.

I dropped below the dashboard just as the vehicle crashed into the line of soldiers. Bodies went flying as I jerked the wheel hard to the right. As I pulled the emergency brake, the van went into a tailspin. The tires shrieked as the armored vehicle lifted from the pavement.

I sucked in a quick breath and leapt along with the momentum of the vehicle. I flew through the air and hit the ground in a roll that caused pain to lash my back. Only as I came to my feet, I grabbed the dropped AK-47 from one of the soldiers and started firing. My first two shots missed their mark, but the third took one in the jaw, sending him sprawling backward onto the asphalt.

The others fanned out to avoid my rounds, their shots going wide as they sprayed bullets in my general direction. The smell of gasoline filled the air as I turned to see a soldier pulling the helicopter's door closed from inside.

No. I couldn't let Llanzo escape! If he got away, Ren's daughter was as good as dead. I couldn't allow that to happen.

I emptied my AK at the hiding soldiers and sprinted toward the helicopter. I caught the landing gear of the helicopter with the crook of my elbow as it left the ground. As the soldiers began to peek out from their hiding places, I swung my legs around the cold metal skid, bracing myself against it as the helicopter lifted into the air and sped through the rapidly opening hatchway in the ceiling.

16

I wasn't quite sure how far they had flown, but I was starting to get tired. Worse, if they didn't land soon, I was going to have to try to take them down midair, and while I'd done that before, the last time, I had a gun, and it had been over water. Now we were over the jungle. There'd be no relatively soft landing if I fell this time. If I waited until the helicopter landed, it'd likely be in a place where Llanzo had more people. That would go south in a hurry. That was a non-plan. No. My only chance was to try to take it now and somehow keep from getting killed or crashing the helicopter.

"The hell with it," I muttered while pulling myself into a standing position on the helicopter's skid. I gripped the door with one hand while pulling my stolen Becker BK2 free of the sheath. I took a deep breath, counted to ten in my head, and hauled the door open.

The closest soldier turned in my direction in time to catch my knife with his throat. As blood spurted from his ruined neck, I grabbed his AK-47 from his hands. I raised the weapon as the helicopter lurched to the side, throwing me from my feet and into the belly of the beast.

I crashed to the ground as the soldier beside Llanzo threw off his seatbelt. As he moved around the immense drug lord and brought his own AK up, I fired.

Bullets ripped through the soldier and Llanzo alike, splintering what remained of my hearing into a ringing cry. As Llanzo slumped forward, choking on his own blood, the helicopter lurched again. I slid toward the still open door as the body of the soldier I'd stabbed slid out into nothingness.

I grabbed onto Llanzo's pant leg with both hands, my feet dangling toward the open door. My muscles strained against gravity as I hung there for what felt like forever.

As the helicopter straightened, the door to the cockpit slid open. A man appeared in the doorway with a pistol in his hands. His eyes widened in shock as I pointed my AK-47 at him and pulled the trigger in a controlled burst. He fell backward in a spray of crimson that hit me in the face, coating me with hot, sticky blood.

I scrambled to my feet and cursed as I looked at Llanzo. He was dead, and because of that, there was no way he could tell me where Annabeth was being kept.

"Dammit!" I cried, nearly throwing down my weapon in frustration, and for a second, I nearly let despair take hold of me. Only, I couldn't give up now. Just because this guy was dead, didn't mean Annabeth was. Surely someone would know where she was. And there was still one person left to talk to. The pilot. I moved across the cabin and pointed my weapon at the pilot through the doorway.

"Don't do anything stupid, or I'll shoot you," I yelled over the wind whipping through the cabin.

"I won't. You just killed my boss, and you have a gun on me," he murmured, not taking his eyes off the scenery outside. Lush green filled the land for miles and miles. Were we somewhere over the middle of the island? Already? "What do you want me to do?"

"I need you to take me to where Llanzo is keeping the Jamaican Wave," I replied.

"I don't know where that is…" He glanced at

me as I slid into the copilot's seat, careful to keep the AK pointed at him. "I'm just the pilot. I go where I'm told."

"Where are we now?" I growled, turning to look back at Llanzo's corpse. Another wave of despair ripped through me. "And where is someone who will know?"

"Right now, we're near Linstead." He took a deep breath and let it out slowly. "We were on our way to Kingston. Would you like to go there…?"

I watched him closely. He was nervous in a way that made me think he was lying to me. "What's in Kingston?"

"Llanzo's safe house is in Kingston. He has a plane there. I was heading there so he could get on it and fly out of Jamaica." The pilot looked at me. "Because of you."

"If he planned of fleeing, why not just go to Sangster International in Montego Bay?" I asked. Something definitely didn't smell right about this story. "A guy like Llanzo has to be able to leave from there."

"He had to meet someone first, but I'm not sure who or why." The pilot sighed. "So where do you want to go?"

The question bugged me. Something was off, I just couldn't put my finger on it.

I turned and looked back at Llanzo while making sure I kept my AK trained on the pilot. Llanzo's bloated, bulbous body sagged against his restraints as blood stained his suit with crimson. Only, the pattern didn't seem quite right. I'd seen enough bullet-riddled corpses in my time with the Marines to know what they looked like, and as I took him in, I realized what was going on.

"Is that what I think it is?" I whipped back around to face the pilot and jammed the gun into his ribs.

"It isn't my fault…" he cried out. His alabaster skin paled as he looked at me.

"That's a decoy, isn't it?" I said, hoping it was true. If it was, while I may have lost time, it meant Llanzo was still out there, and if he was out there, I could find him and make him tell me where Ren's daughter was.

"I'm sorry. Please… please don't shoot me," the pilot said, swallowing hard.

"Take me back, or there will be consequences you will not like," I said, turning once more to look at the corpse in the fat suit. It was good enough that

I hadn't noticed it at first. Hell, I probably wouldn't have noticed if he hadn't been shot full of holes.

"You don't seem as upset as I thought you'd be," the pilot said as he whirled the helicopter around and began heading back.

"If he's not dead, I can find him, and if I can find him, I can find my friend's daughter," I said, hoping he hadn't escaped. I wasn't sure how much time I'd lost by following the decoy, but hopefully, it wasn't enough for him to escape. There was just one problem. How was I going to find him now? Worse, if I didn't, what would happen to Ren's daughter?

Llanzo had to be heading somewhere, and while I had lost some time, I just needed to find where that somewhere was. I turned back to the pilot and stared at him for a long moment.

"Where was your boss is going?" I asked, pushing the AK into his ribs again. "It probably goes without saying, but if you don't tell me, I'll throw you from a moving helicopter a mile above a jungle." I nodded toward the lush greenery outside the window. "If I were you, I'd decide soon. This thing has a hair trigger, and who knows what turbulence we'll hit?"

17

As we flew back over the Montego Room, I quickly realized that even if Llanzo was down there, I'd never get to him because the place would be crawling with police. A surge of annoyance shot through me. Even if they'd found the secret drug lab and whatnot below the facility, the likeliest scenario was that Llanzo had flown the coop.

"If he's not down there, where is he?" I asked, gesturing offhandedly toward the police cars outside the club.

"Do you want me to guess?" the pilot asked, completing his last sweep of the area.

"Might as well," I huffed and leaned my head against the chair. "It's got to be better than mine."

"Maybe at his home?" the pilot said, shrugging. "If he's not there, then I really have no idea."

"We may as well check," I said, hoping Llanzo hadn't just skipped town already. For all I knew, he was on a plane on his way to Brazil right now.

"It's not far, we'll be there in a couple minutes," the pilot replied, angling the helicopter around and jetting through the crisp blue skies.

He was right. Only a few minutes later, I found myself staring down at a gated community right at the edge of the beach. Huge mansions filled the entire community, but the truly interesting thing was that as we moved closer, there was a second gated area within the original community.

"A second gate? What's that for?" I asked, pointing at it as we passed over it.

"That's so the truly wealthy do not have to sully themselves by being around those who are only well off," the pilot replied with a shrug. "You'll find this often in Jamaica. Rich foreigners building sprawling wealthy communities designed to keep the local riffraff away."

"Seems excessive," I muttered, but at the same time, I'd known more than a few rich people. While most were nice enough, there were some who used their money to keep everyone else away. It wasn't surprising that the same thing had happened on these pristine beaches too.

"That is Llanzo's house," the pilot said, pointing out a large home at the back of the area overlooking the beach. A huge wall surrounded it, letting me know it'd be even more difficult to break into, but not impossible. Besides, most of the houses around here seemed to be vacation homes, which meant there'd be fewer people around in general. That always made sneaking around easier.

"Thanks," I said, nodding to the pilot. "I appreciate the help. Can you land this somewhere nearby?"

"There's a helicopter tour company not too far away. I can put it down on their helipad. I've done it lots of times. It's no big deal." He glanced around down below. "There's nowhere inside where I can land it."

"That should work…" I mumbled, hoping the pilot had actually shown me the right house. If he hadn't this could end badly for me.

A few moments later, we had landed behind a chain-link gate. There were no other vehicles, and no one came out to greet us. Helicopter tour company, my ass.

"Is this where you kill me?" the pilot asked as

the skids touched the concrete helipad, and he powered down the rotors. "If it is, I think my wife and kids would appreciate it if you left my face alone…"

"I don't think so," I said, getting to my feet. "At least not yet. I want to be able to come back and talk to you if you lied to me about Llanzo's house."

"Fair enough," the guy replied before muttering something under his breath. His gold wedding band flashed in the light as he angled around to look at me. "You might think I'm a bad guy, but we all have bills."

"Get up and lay down in the back," I said, ignoring his comment. "Hurry up, or I'm going to go with option two." I took a step back to allow him room to move. "That's where I shoot you."

The pilot stood without another word and moved to the back of the helicopter.

"Thanks," he murmured as I pulled out the handcuffs I'd removed from one of the dead soldiers before I'd tossed his body into the jungle.

I knelt next to him and cuffed his hands around the seat's support. Then I knocked him unconscious with a quick blow from the Beretta I'd taken from the same soldier. As the pilot slumped into unconsciousness, I stood and looked down at him.

"I really hope this doesn't bite me in the ass," I said before turning and exiting the helicopter.

I made my way to the chain-link fence surrounding the otherwise innocuous stretch of asphalt and grumbled when I reached the gate because it was locked with not one, but two locks. Both were heavy duty devices, and while one sported a keyhole I could probably get through if I searched the pilot, the other was a combination lock.

"Dammit," I murmured as I looked up at the top of the fence. It was covered in rusty razor wire. Sighing, I moved back toward the helicopter and pulled one of the parachute packs off the wall inside the cabin. Then I made my way over to the closest stretch of fence. I climbed up it and used the parachute pack to push down the razor-wire and crawl over the top.

I threw one last look back at the pilot as I flung the shredded parachute into the bushes beside the gate before making my way toward the buildings a few blocks away.

A few minutes away, I was standing next to a red and green roofed restaurant boasting ten different ways to eat conch.

Thankfully, it only took a couple minutes for me

to spot a taxi, and as I waved frantically at it, the driver seemed to notice me. The green and white sedan pulled up next to me, and a black male with cornrows and a Rastafarian T-shirt, leaned toward the open passenger window.

"Where do you want to go?" he asked, voice surprisingly friendly. "I'm not like the other drivers, I can give you a good price if it's far away."

"I need to go to St. James," I said, and the guy's eyebrows went up a notch.

"St. James, eh? That's a flat rate price." He paused and rubbed his chin. Then he quoted a price that made me think I was getting ripped off.

"That's fine," I said, and the guy nodded, leaping from his vehicle and coming around to open my door. As I settled into the cab's backseat, the driver got back into his seat and headed toward Llanzo's mansion.

Fifteen minutes later, I stood about half a block away from the gated community. As the taxi driver took off, leaving me to my own devices, I made my way toward the gates, on the lookout for anyone suspicious. So far, I hadn't seen anything. Hell, I hadn't even seen any police, but given recent events, I was betting most of them were down at the Montego Room.

The front walk had a couple floodlights, but since it was daytime, they weren't on. From where I stood, I saw a pair of video cameras outside the gated community, but the two guards in the bungalow outside the gate looked to be too busy playing cards and drinking coffee to pay them much mind. Still, the direct approach was likely to have me both caught on camera and stopped.

"Maybe I could wait for a car to go inside and follow along?" I mused, but as I stared at the guards in their air-conditioned bungalow, I dismissed the idea. They'd definitely stop me if they saw me trying to sneak in, and once again, I'd likely be seen by the video cameras.

No. It was time to think of a different way. I made my way past the gate and headed toward the beach. I wasn't sure, but maybe it was possible to swim around the gate without being seen?

"Damn," I muttered after I'd walked a half a block to the beach. Sitting just on the edge of the sand was another bungalow with two more guards and more cameras, likely to deter anyone from doing what I wanted to do. That combined with the netting stretching out to a buoy about a hundred yards out, let me know I wasn't getting in that way.

"Think, Billy," I muttered to myself as I moved

back toward the street, anxiety starting to well up inside me. I had to find a way inside and fast. If I didn't, who knew what would happen to Annabeth?

As I stepped onto the sidewalk and cast an annoyed glance at the gate, something caught my eye, and a really bad plan sprung to mind. I spun on my heel and jogged back along the road until I got to the corner and hung a right toward the beach. A few hundred yards away, I found exactly what I wanted. An unguarded manhole cover on a vacant stretch of road hidden by lush foliage.

I made my way over to it and pulled out my Becker BK2. I knelt beside the cover and set to work on it with the knife, thankful it was designed to pry off a car door. That said, the blade was short, and I didn't have a lot of leverage, so it took me a lot of grunting and swearing to lift the manhole cover. That done, I climbed inside and pulled the cover back into place. Darkness enveloped me, and the smell and humidity of the sewer rushed up to greet me like an old friend.

Resisting both the urge to hold my breath and vomit at the same time, I pulled out the small LED flashlight I'd taken from the soldier on the helicopter and flipped it on. Holding it in one hand, I made my way down the metal rungs of the ladder set into the wall and hopped onto the ground.

Sludge covered my sandals in an instant, and as the smell worsened, I decided not to look down at my feet. No good could come from that. Instead, I focused on the task at hand, infiltrate Llanzo's mansion, find him, and make him give up Annabeth's location.

I moved back along the tunnel, doing my best to estimate my way to the gated community by peering up through storm drains.

When my innate sense of direction started pinging, telling me I was far enough into the community to risk getting out, I moved to the next manhole and climbed up the ladder. I pushed, pressing my palms against the heavy steel lid with all the strength I could muster. My arm and back muscles strained and corded, but thankfully I was able to slide it up. I peered out around the street, thankful I was actually inside the gated community. Even better, I could see the secondary gate about a block behind me.

Hefting the lid out of the way, I crawled out onto the street. After moving the manhole cover back into place, I wiped my sandals off on the asphalt, trying as best I could to get the squelching muck off.

Satisfied they weren't going to squish at the wrong moment and give me away, or worse, make me slip and fall, I moved toward where I'd seen Llanzo's house during my brief aerial tour of the community. Every step I took made me glad most of these mansions were unoccupied vacation homes.

After only a few minutes, I turned the corner and stared at Llanzo's home. A ten-foot-tall, black wrought-iron fence surrounded the entire property, making it so I couldn't glimpse much behind it. Even still, I could tell the two-story mansion was huge. Like most of the buildings I'd seen on the island, this one appeared to be made of cement too. Though these walls had the stamped concrete look to them.

Unlike the rest of the mansions, it was full of activity. Two well-dressed sentries stood beside the wrought iron gate at the front of the property, heads constantly scanning for passersby. What I could see of the rest of the compound revealed even more guards, but what's more, I spotted a black Humvee similar to the ones I'd seen inside the Montego Room bunker.

Crouching down behind one of the neighbor's bushes, I took a moment to watch the sentries. After about fifteen or so minutes, I noticed an irregularity, albeit a tiny one. If I moved quickly, I'd be able to take down the right guard before his partner noticed. There was just one problem. I'd have to get up close and personal to do it. If I used my gun, I could probably get both of them from here, but that would also alert the entire compound to an attack.

As the right guard completed his circuit around the perimeter and turned back toward the gate, I sprinted forward. My chest heaved as I crashed into him, one hand wrapping around his mouth while the other slipped the blade of the Becker across his throat. Blood spilled down the front of him as his hands went to the wound. As I dropped the gurgling guard to the pavement, I stepped past him and flung the heavy knife at the left guard who had turned away to watch the other side of the yard.

As the heavy blade caught him in the back of the neck, I was already sprinting toward him. His head jerked forward, and as he stumbled, I sprang into the air. My knees crashed into his back as I rode him down to the floor while using both my hands to shove his face into the cement. His nose shattered in a spray of blood as he hit, and I reared back to hit him if he so much as twitched.

Fortunately, he was unconscious, and I spared a

quick second to frisk him. My heart did a little leap of joy when I found a silenced Beretta on his person, complete with one of the super-extended twenty round magazines.

When his body revealed no other weaponry, I moved quickly, dragging him and his partner back behind the bushes I'd watched them from. I took another moment to calm myself before moving toward the compound once more.

A quick glance through the gate revealed four more guards in the courtyard, but unlike the men I'd just fought, these were all holding AK-47s. It made me wonder if the drug dealer had been hesitant to show that kind of hardware outside his house despite the street being nearly deserted.

I moved along the wall, careful to stay hidden even though it was unlikely they'd see me through the tightly packed wrought-iron beams. They seemed to follow a standard route much like the two outside had, and it didn't take long to figure out.

Leaning toward the gate, I raised my Beretta and sighted on the first guard. Four quick shots later, all four of them were corpses on the ground. I shoved the Beretta in the shoulder holster I'd taken from the guard, grabbed the top of the fence and hauled myself up and over.

As my feet touched the soft grass on the other side of the wall, I saw how nice the house actually was. It was only two stories but had huge brick columns supporting a pair of expansive second-floor balconies that overlooked a massive pool with a huge rock waterfall on one side and a swim-up bar on the other.

Worried a bullet would come from an unseen guard, I darted across the lawn, pausing only to scoop up one of the dead guard's assault rifles. I slung it over my shoulder before making my way around the property just in case there were other guards. Thankfully, there weren't, and even better the quick walk around the property revealed a way inside.

The guest room right above the pillar on the far back corner of the house was dark. Moving over to it, I grabbed hold of the bricks and pulled myself up. My muscles strained as I grabbed each crevice and shimmied inch by inch up it.

By the time I pulled myself over the ledge and onto the balcony's floor, I was exhausted. Much harder than I'd expected and the Jamaican heat and humidity hadn't helped things. I couldn't think about that, so I pulled the Beretta from its holster and leaned against the wall to listen.

Hearing nothing, I moved forward and tried the sliding glass door that led onto the balcony. It opened with barely any effort, and I thanked my lucky stars they were careless enough to leave it unlocked.

I stepped into a room with that tile that was supposed to look like cherry wood and marveled at the expense of it. The paintings on the walls had to have been worth twice what the house was. A massive four-poster bed straight out of the Victorian age took up most of the space inside the room. As I made my way past it toward the hallway door, I readied my weapon and leaned against the door, listening for movement.

I could hear at least two men on either end of the hallway, probably one guarding the stairs to the second floor while the other was guarding Llanzo's room. Going out there would put me in a shooting gallery.

Worse, if I opened the door, while I might be able to take out one or both of the guards, there could be more. Call me crazy, but I didn't think this thin bedroom door was going to do much to stop them once they knew where I was. No, I had to find another way.

18

As I stared at the bathroom on my right, an idea popped into my head. I edged closer and pushed the ornate wooden door open. The room was all Grecian marble and gold filigree with a separate shower and a huge Jacuzzi tub.

Shutting the door to mask any noise, I stuffed towels against the overflow drain in the tub. Then as quietly as I could manage, I turned on the water. I stood there staring at it, counting the seconds until it reached the halfway point.

"This is it," I mumbled to myself as I made my way back out to the balcony.

As I moved to the far corner, I stared at the gap between this balcony and the next. It was maybe three feet, and while I wasn't sure if it was actually the master bedroom on the other side, the commotion I saw through the curtains made me think it might very well be. Better still, no one had come outside to check on the downed guards, so the coast was clear.

"No time like the present," I said as I climbed onto the railing.

I sprang from the railing, leaping across the gap and grabbing onto the railing for the next balcony. My arms jerked hard in their sockets, and I stifled a cry of pain before pulling myself over the railing and into the balcony. I unslung my AK-47 as I crept over to the wall beside the sliding glass doors and waited.

It didn't take long. The lights in the guest room turned on, spilling light onto the balcony as men rushed in. Ignoring them, I crouched down and edged forward to look inside the bedroom beside me. While I could make out four men behind the curtains, I wasn't quite sure who was who. One stood by the door to the hallway while two more were crowded around a third man. That had to be Llanzo.

I pointed the weapon at the three men, silently

counted to five, and let loose two bursts of fire that shattered the glass doors. My ears rang from the report of the machinegun as the two guys in front slid to the floor while the third dove for cover. I ignored him as I brought the rifle around and fired at the guard at the door.

The bullets caught him mid-turn, tearing through his side and pitching him into the hallway. Shouts filled my ears as I stepped through the shattered doors. Glass crunched beneath my sandals as I pushed aside the curtain and surveyed the wreckage.

A man who looked like the fat man I'd killed on the helicopter was huddled on the ground behind the bodies of two dark-skinned soldiers trying his best to appear invisible despite his bulk. Blood leaked from holes in his shoulders as he screamed for help.

More shouts erupted from the hallway, and I knew men would start pouring through the door any second. I fired another burst from the AK-47 into the wall of the room while I sprinted toward Llanzo. Bullets tore through the drywall and splintered the doorway as I slid to a stop beside the drug lord.

"Please," he grunted through clenched teeth. "Whatever they are paying you, I can double, no quadruple it."

"I don't want your money," I snarled, pulling the Beretta free of its holster and pointing it at his face while keeping my AK on the doorway. "I just want information."

"Please, anything. Whatever you want to know, I'll tell you," he squealed, tears and snot running down his face as he spoke. Then the smell of his bowels releasing hit me, and I had to restrain myself from shooting him. This coward had kidnapped my friend's daughter and who knew how many others. He'd run drugs and had people killed, and now, when faced with his death, he couldn't even face it like a man? Pathetic.

"I want to know what your people did with the Jamaican Wave—a tour boat. Your people took it." I jammed the barrel of the Beretta into his forehead, pushing his head backward. "Where is it?"

"Wh-what?" he asked, confusion filling his features as I put a blast into the wall of the guest room and hallway. Men cried out as bodies hit the floor. While I wasn't sure if I'd actually hit anyone, I was sure they'd at least taken cover. That'd buy me a few more seconds.

"The Jamaican Wave," I snarled, turning back to it. "My friend's daughter was on board. Where is it?"

The sounds of footsteps filled my ears as Llanzo looked at me dumbly. He was starting to go into shock. That wasn't good. I emptied the AK into the walls, trying to gain a few more seconds. As it went empty, I tossed the spent rifle to the floor and snatched up one of the dead guard's submachine guns. As I lifted the weapon, a head appeared low in the doorway, but a quick burst of gunfire reduced it to a smudge on the wall.

"I… I don't know where the Jamaican Wave is," Llanzo said when I turned back to him.

"Then what good are you?" I asked right before I shot him in the thigh. He screamed, but I ignored it. "Tell me where she is!"

"I already handed them all off," he said, the hope in his eyes all but dying as he spoke. "They were all to board the Tidal Wave at the docks."

"Where was the Tidal Wave taking them?" I asked, glancing from the doorway to him and back again. I could hear people moving around outside, and I knew it wouldn't be long before they started shooting at me. Hell, the only thing that kept them from doing it was that they probably didn't want to shoot their boss.

"To a plane out a mile or so." He swallowed hard and then told me the coordinates.

"Why are they being brought out to a plane?" I asked.

"They've been sold as slaves to Abbad Tehan. He has certain… proclivities he likes to explore…" Llanzo shivered, and the look on his face made revulsion and anger well up inside me.

"I'm not sure how you could sell a couple of girls to someone like that, but it's not my job to judge," I said right before I put a bullet in his brain. "I just arrange the meeting."

As his body slumped lifelessly to the floor, I edged backward toward the balcony in a crouch, careful to keep my Uzi trained on the doorway. The moment my back touched the curtains, I spun around and moved out past the shattered glass doors, Careful to keep my body shielded by the railing.

Sirens filled the air while men scurried inside the house, no doubt readying themselves for a charge. The moment they realized Llanzo was dead, they'd come for me, guns blazing.

I needed an escape and fast if I had any hope

of reaching the Tidal Wave before its rendezvous with the plane. As I tried to think of an escape plan, my eyes settled on the pool.

"Here goes nothing," I whispered under my breath as I spun back around and unloaded two more volleys. My first burst shredded the master bedroom while the other sprayed the balcony of the guestroom. I wasn't taking any chances someone was out there waiting for me to pop out of cover.

I took off at a full sprint and dove over the railing. I hit the pool a half a second later, and as cold washed over me, hot lead tore through the water around me. As my feet touched the bottom of the pool, I kicked off, angling toward the stairs. My lungs burned for air as I twisted around and pulled my Beretta from its holster. As I set my sights on the soldier leaning over the balcony of the guestroom, I burst through the surface, firing my Uzi.

A lucky shot caught the soldier in the shoulder. A scream tore from his lips as the bullet spun him into his still reloading partner. They crashed to the ground out of sight as I sprinted up the stairs and onto dry land. I backed toward the compound's wall, firing until the Uzi clicked empty.

I dropped the weapon, spun around, and grabbed hold of the wall. I hauled myself up and over it so quickly I scraped the flesh from my hands. As I dropped down on the other side, bullets began chewing up the ornate wrought-iron.

Instead of firing back, I sprinted down the block before disappearing into the yard of an unlit mansion. My chest heaved as I dropped behind a cluster of rose bushes and watched Llanzo's compound. As a man came sprinting out into the open and glanced around, submachinegun at the ready, I lined him up in my sights. I pulled the trigger three times in rapid succession. My shots caught him center mass.

He staggered backward, his gun slipping from his hands as I turned and raced toward the side door on the side of the mansion's garage. I put a bullet into the jam, splintering the wood around the lock before kicking it as hard as I could. The door burst inward in a spray of debris, and as I moved inside, my mouth fell open.

"Well, I'll be a monkey's uncle," I muttered, eyeing the hot pink Ferrari sitting unattended and lonely next to a Rolls Royce Ghost. Who the hell left over half a million dollars' worth of cars sitting in an unattended vacation home?

That was pretty much when the alarm went off, blaring so loudly, it shattered my hearing.

"Dammit," I cursed, looking around for the alarm box. Embedded into the wall beside the alarm panel was a steel lockbox that reminded me of the ones used to store keys. I raced toward it and pulled on the handle, but it was locked. I put my Beretta to the mechanism and fired a round into it. The next time I pulled on it, the door opened. Keys filled my eyes, and I snatched the Ferrari's and turned toward the vehicle.

I used the fob to unlock it before grabbing the door and flinging it open. As I slid into the seat, gunfire erupted from beyond the garage, perforating the metal, but I ignored it as I turned the key. The car roared to life like an avenging god.

I hit the button on the remote clipped to the visor causing the garage door to lift. Then I shifted into reverse and stomped on the gas. The car rocketed backward as I ducked down. I raced out into the open, surprising the four men standing on the sidewalk outside.

They dove to the side as I hit the street in a flurry of sparks. Before they could recover, I shifted the car into gear while spinning the vehicle into a turn that made the tires squeal.

The Ferrari's engine roared as I drove down the block and approached the secondary gate. When I got within twenty feet of it, the red light on the side turned green, and the gate began to swing open. Evidently, it wasn't designed to keep people inside. Good.

I gunned it, bursting through the gate the second it was wide enough to let me through, then turned onto a street leading back toward the main entrance. Once I was outside, I'd be on my way to the docks. I just had to get there in time.

The RPMs shot into the red zone as I raced toward the main entrance in time to see red and blue lights strobing in the distance. They were headed straight toward the gated community.

"Screw it," I said and floored it.

The security guards shouted at me, waving at me to stop as I took a deep breath and braced for impact. Only, just like before, when I got within twenty feet, the gate began to slowly open.

I slammed into the still-opening wrought-iron gate a second later, tearing the mirrors from the Ferrari's frame in a flurry of sparks. The gates groaned, their springs buckling as they snapped outward at disjointed angles.

The impact shuddered through my body, and I struggled to control of the Ferrari as it lurched to the side. I jerked hard on the wheel, barely avoiding the lead police car as I left the road. Dirt and grass flew everywhere as I maneuvered the vehicle across the well-manicured lawn.

The rest of the police slammed on their brakes as I spun the vehicle while hitting the gas. It shot back onto the road. The Ferrari smashed through the front of a police car and very nearly stopped. Then the screeching tires caught hold of the street, and the 480-plus horsepower engine sent me rocketing forward.

Angling down the street away from the police, I heard the telltale sounds of a helicopter. I whipped around a corner, then made another hard left before hitting the brakes. As the Ferrari slowed, I leapt from the vehicle.

I hit the lush foliage beside the sidewalk with bone-shuddering force and tried my best to duck and roll through it. By the time I came to a stop across the sidewalk, my bones ached, and my skin felt raw. As I pushed it down and scrambled to my feet, the Ferrari careened forward. It slammed into a fire hydrant and ripped it free in a spray of water before spinning haphazardly and shearing through the glass window of a scuba shop.

After shaking my head for a second to clear the cobwebs, I sprinted down the alleyway beside the scuba shop and clambered up and over the chain-link fence at the back. I hit the ground on the other side in a dead run. A moment later, I was on a street filled with tourists, street vendors, and various other people, none of whom paid me any attention.

I looked around, desperate for a place to go and spotted a shabby looking hotel up the block with a pair of taxis in front. I fast walked toward it as casually as possible, doing my best to blend in with the crowd as the police helicopter circled overhead. Only it was way more interested in the wreckage of the Ferrari than it was of the street I was on.

Despite the sirens wailing on the street a block over, I arrived in front of the closest taxi a moment later relatively unscathed and knocked on the window. It came down to reveal an overweight black man with a gray beard and a bald head. He smiled at me, revealing a gold tooth.

"Need a ride?" he asked, looking me up and down. "To a hospital maybe?"

"Actually, I wanna go to the docks. Can you take me there?" I asked, pulling a pair of twenties from my pocket and holding them up. "You can keep the change if you make it snappy."

"Buddy, I'd stab my own mother for that kind

of scratch." He nodded at me and unlocked the doors. "Get in. We'll be there in ten minutes."

"Thanks," I said, sliding into the backseat. I didn't even have myself buckled in before we were on the street and heading away from the blaring sirens and strobing lights.

19

W e'd barely been on the road for a few minutes when my phone rang. My hand went to my pocket, and I pulled out the device. Max was calling.

"Hello?" I said, hitting the answer button as the taxi driver wove through the busy streets.

"Billy, we're here. Sorry about the wait," Max said, and I could hear the wind whipping around in the background. "We're at the docks. I don't know what you've been up to, but Montego Bay is way too hot for us to come ashore with our kind of hardware. It's touchy as it is."

"Wait a second," I said, hoping I'd heard him correctly. If he was at the docks, I just might make it in time to save Annabeth. "What do you mean you're at the docks?"

"Well, I figured we were going after a boat, so I got us a boat," Max said, suddenly concerned. "Or am I wrong? I mean, I can come on shore, if you need me too…"

"No, that's perfect!" I said and began relaying him the information I'd gleaned thus far while being careful not to say anything the taxi driver might think odd. Fortunately, the guy was way too busy singing along to his music to pay me much mind.

"Okay, I'll get everything ready for the trip. The Princess Pearl is pretty quick, so depending on what they have, we might make it. I'll also have Vicky start scanning for a seaplane at those coordinates. She's good at those computer things. Not Ren good, but better than me. I can barely work my phone." He laughed.

"Say, speaking of Ren, have you heard from him? Every time I call I get his voicemail, which makes no sense since it's his daughter we're trying to save."

"Nope, not since he relayed us the information. I know he was in deep cover, so maybe he's having trouble getting away," Max asked, and I hesitated for a minute. "You're right though. Ren would move mountains for his girl. Let me see if someone can check on him. Just to be on the safe side. We're at dock six, slip four. Give me a call when you're here."

A few minutes later, I'd paid the cabbie and stepped out of the car. The scenery surrounding the parking lot for the docks was filled with palm trees that reached high up into the sky, and as the cab sped off down the main drag from the visitor drop off area, I realized there was only one squat wooden booth.

An old man sat just inside of it behind a small electric fan. He was reading a magazine, and as I stared at him, I realized that it was an information booth designed to sell tours to tourists. I turned away from it and looked back at the docks.

They were surprisingly well kept, probably because they were surrounded by a huge chain-link fence with razor-wire over the top. Beyond the fence, I could see a variety of boats moored there. Everything from fishing boats to giant yachts with tables set across the decks for dinner cruises.

Fortunately, while there weren't any people waiting to get inside, someone had propped the gate to my left open with a two by four. Probably a dock worker who was having to go back and forth between the many delivery vans on that side of the parking lot and one of the yachts.

As I made my way toward the open gate, part of me was amazed I'd made it here so easily after the firefight, but I was betting the cops were too busy with the corpse of Llanzo's empire to pay me much attention. For the moment, anyway.

I pulled out my phone and dialed Max's number as I passed through the gate and headed toward dock six. He answered just as I reached it.

"Is that you, Billy?" he asked, and I saw a figure on a boat all the way at the end raise a hand and wave at me. "Do you see me?"

"I'm here," I said, waving back. "I'll be there in a minute."

"Sounds good," he said, and the phone clicked off. A moment later I was standing in front of a twenty-six-foot motorboat with Princess Pearl stenciled onto the side in black. I looked it up and down as Max came over to the side and looked down at me.

He was a barrel-chested man clad in a black, sweat-wicking polo shirt, Bermuda shorts, and a captain's hat. He smiled, the scars on his face stretching across his features as he reached out to help me up.

As I took his hand, I couldn't help but stare at the scars on his face. It almost looked like he'd been clawed by a wildcat, and I knew from experience that they ran down beneath the collar of his shirt and down his chest and back. He'd told me it was from a fight with a tiger out in Indonesia, and while he had no reason to lie to me, I never quite believed the tale.

"What kind of boat is this?" I asked, putting my foot on the side of the boat while he helped haul my ass on board. "I've never seen anything like it before. It's sort of like a Fiberform Command Bridge Cruiser, but they don't have a backend like this one."

"Yeah, I doubt you have," Max replied, smacking the wall of the cockpit with one hand. "It's a custom job," he added, but when he didn't elaborate further, I decided not to press. As long as it was fast and didn't sink, I was good. "You ready?"

"Yeah," I said as Max clapped me on the shoulder, forcing me to look at him. "What is it?"

"You know, your Mary Ann is a hell of a girl," he said, making eye contact with me, and something about the way he looked at me made me pause.

"And...?" I asked, arching an eyebrow.

Before he could respond, the cockpit opened to

reveal Mary Ann standing there at the wheel. She wore black and pink active wear that hugged her athletic body, and as I stared at her in shock, she looked me up and down, her sapphire eyes taking everything in.

"I made him take me," she said, eyes sparkling with annoyance. "Although you should have just agreed to let me come." She shook her head. "I don't know why you'd think I'd miss this opportunity—"

Before she could say more, I rushed over, sweeping her up in my arms. "I just didn't want you to get hurt," I whispered. "But I missed you so much."

"Wait, you're not mad?" she asked, momentarily stunned.

I kissed her then, pressing my lips against hers. When we finally broke out kiss, I leaned my forehead against hers. "No, I'm not mad. There's no one else I'd rather have at my back."

She nodded, a flash of emotion rippling through her sapphire eyes before fading behind a mask of embarrassment as she turned away from me. "Billy, you keep saying things like that and I'll fall in love with you all over again." She shook her head, taking a moment to compose herself. "I've got the coordinates locked in." She gestured back toward the cockpit. "I'll get us on the way if you and Max want to hammer out a plan?"

"Sounds good," Max said, throwing off the last of the dock lines. His eyes turned back to me, all business. "Come on, I have some toys you might be interested in."

"Probably best if you get out of sight, anyway, Billy." Mary Ann glanced over her shoulder at me. "You have a way of kicking hornet nests."

"I'd do as she says," Max affirmed, moving toward a hatch set into the ground and hoisting it open with one hand to reveal stairs that led into the depths of the boat. "I've learned to never argue with pretty ladies."

"Words to live by," I said, following him down the stairs. It was much bigger than I'd have expected from my cursory glance around the boat. While it wasn't furnished, it wasn't sparse either. A pair of tables sat along the far wall in front of a wide bench.

"If you're mad about your girl, you need to take it up with her, not me," Max said, shutting the overhead door. "Understand?"

"I understand," I said as the boat lurched forward. I did too. Max was a simple person, and he hated drama. The fact that Mary Ann had gotten him to take her along, knowing I'd be annoyed spoke volumes.

"I know you do, Billy," Max replied as he moved toward the table and gestured at it. Clothes and weapons covered it. "Not let's get this over with."

"I really will help you with something after this is over," I added as I grabbed an overhead hand-hold for stability. As the boat settled out, I made my way toward the table and flopped down on the bench next to Max.

"Don't worry about it, Billy," Max said, staring out the small porthole toward the steadily disappearing island of Jamaica. "I mean that. Let's just get Ren's girl back."

"All right," I said as I reached across the table and began going through the assorted gear.

20

"Um, guys," Mary Ann said through the crackling loudspeaker overhead. "You need to get up here now."

"What's going on?" I asked, glancing at Max who shook his head at me.

"Not sure," he said, springing to his feet and depressing the button beside the speaker. "What's going on, Mary Ann?"

I was already on my feet, heading toward the exit. I knew that tone. It meant trouble.

"I found the plane…" There was a pause as I moved up the ladder and pushed the doors open. The burst of gunfire from outside drowned out her words.

The Tidal Wave sat a little ways off lashed to what looked like a floating dock. It was crawling with men sporting automatic weapons, but that wasn't the problem. No. The problem was that two speedboats loaded with more men were coming toward us. Fast.

Worse, the DHC-6 Twin Otter seaplane's propellers were already spinning as the men on the docks, struggled to load it. White foam sprayed out beneath it, and I knew that we had only moments before they finished loading the plane and lifted into the air.

"You get the plane, Billy," Max said, clapping me on the shoulder and forcibly pushing me up onto the deck of the ship. "I'll get the boat."

"How am I going to get the plane?" I asked, turning to look at him.

Instead of responding, he pushed past me and flung open the door to the cockpit. "Mary Ann, set us for intercept."

"On it," she said, gunning the engine and causing water to spray out the back of our boat. We surged forward over the crest of a wave and slammed down hard into the ocean as the speedboats opened fire, the Browning M2 machineguns spitting rounds at the Princess Pearl.

We dove for cover as bullets pinged off the hull and, somehow, ricocheted off. "How in the hell?" I murmured, wondering why the boat hadn't just been cut in half. Evidently, whatever made up this boat was tough.

"Max, you didn't answer my question. How am I going to 'get' a goddamned airplane?" I said, frustration welling up inside me.

"We'll get close, and you use this." He shoved a grappling hook into my hands. "You've got one shot so make it count."

I stared down at the weapon in my hands. Then I turned my gaze back to Max. "You think it will work?"

"It doesn't hurt to try. Now get a move on," he replied, before pushing the blue cushion up off the bench beside us and revealing a Barrett M90 sniper rifle. He pulled it and a box of .50 caliber rounds out of the bench before pulling the cushion back in place and clambering on top of it.

As he sighted his sniper rifle on the left speedboat, it fired again. He ducked back down as bullets tore into the boat. Mary Ann swerved, cutting a hard left on the boat and throwing a spray of water into the air. The engines screamed, launching us forward as more bullets peppered the Princess Pearl. Round after round smacked into the cockpit, and while most of them fell uselessly to the ground or ricocheted off, I could tell it wouldn't last long at this rate.

"We have to stop those guns," I said, turning to Max as he dropped off the bench and onto the ground beside me.

"I know that," he said as we hit a bump that had us crashing down hard on the ocean. The force of the impact rattled up into my bones as Max looked at me and pointed toward the back of the boat. "Untie that line."

I turned to see a pair of blue lines tied to the back of the boat, and I turned, trying to crawl toward them as Max moved to the spot I'd occupied and slid a piece of the hull back. He pointed the Barrett out the hole and fired. The sound was a thunder clap and one of the Browning M2s stopped spitting lead at us.

Max reloaded and fired again, clearing the second gunner as the speedboats got closer to us. "Go! I've got you covered."

Trusting him, I scrambled to my feet and got to the lines. They were lashed on with a pair of carabiners, but because whatever was in the ocean had too much drag, I couldn't get them off.

"You really want this off?" I asked, glancing back at Max as his rifle boomed again.

"Yes!" he snapped at me as he reloaded. The speedboats were firing on us again, only now it was small arms fire from cover. Bullets zinged by me as I pulled out my SOG Aegis Mini and used the serrated edge to saw through the right line. It came free and whipped off into the water, making the boat lurch violently onto its left side. I staggered, grabbing onto the guardrail as the engine whined in protest.

"Hurry, Billy!" Max said before his sniper rifle boomed again, throwing someone on the right speed boat into the ocean.

I slashed the last line, and as it whipped free of the boat, the Twin Otter's engines roared, and it started forward.

"It's getting away," I said right before I saw a thin pink filament whip out from under the boat and snap. As it did, whatever I'd cut free exploded, throwing a geyser of water between us and the speedboats. The shockwave threw me backward and I crashed into the bench next to Max as the two speedboats swerved. As they did, Max put a round directly into the guy piloting the left boat's skull.

When his headless corpse dropped to the deck, the boat spun violently out of control. Only it didn't matter because the other speed boat was nearly on us.

I pulled my M16 and fired on it as their rounds forced me to take cover. Bullets pinged off the Princess Pearl, and since they were on the other side, Max couldn't do anything about it. Two men leapt from the speedboat and landed on the front deck as he maneuvered toward the port hole on the other side of the Princess Pearl.

They sprinted for the cockpit, going directly for Mary Ann. I sprang to my feet to give chase, and nearly got my head blown off. I dropped back onto the deck as cover fire turned the area above my head into a kill zone.

"No!" I cried, firing my M16 at them, and pinning down the left one. Only it didn't matter because the right one had what looked like a grenade. He pulled the pin as our boat turned hard to the right. The guy lost his footing, toppling backward over the guardrail into the sea right before the grenade exploded, throwing a bloody geyser into the air.

Max's Barrett thundered, and I glanced back to see he'd gotten back into position. His shot had dropped the enemy pilot, causing the speedboat to veer away.

The report rang in my ears. I leapt to my feet and leapt over to him while firing to keep the last guy who had boarded our ship pinned down. He fired back at me. I ducked for cover as his gun clicked empty. I raised my M16 as he launched himself at me.

His shoulder crashed into my midsection, knocking me onto my back. His left fist came down hard, smashing into my face and making my vision blurry. He reared back to hit me again and the top of his face evaporated into fine red mist. The rumble of Max's Colt Anaconda filled my ears as the dead man slumped forward on top of me.

"We're almost there, Billy! This is your chance!" Max called as I pushed the corpse off of me. I climbed over him and moved to the front of the boat. Salty spray splashed over my skin as machinegun fire erupted from the Tidal Wave.

Bullets pinged off the boat, but I ignored it because I was shielded by the cockpit. Instead, I grabbed the grappling hook off the deck and attached its straps to my arm and chest before holding the weapon out and aiming it at the Twin Otter. The digital readout on the back of the device flashed red, indicating we were still too far away.

"Get ready," Mary Ann cried as the engines

roared and we burst forward quicker than we had any right too. Wind whipped across my face, bringing tears to my eyes.

"I don't suppose you have anything to stop the plane?" I cried, glaring at the grappling hook. It was still flashing, and now the plane was moving forward. At this rate, it'd be a speck in the sky long before we got close enough for me to hit it.

"Can't risk it. If we do, we might kill the people inside," Mary Ann yelled over the pounding surf. "Just get ready. I'm going to try something stupid."

I was about to ask her what she meant by that when the entire boat rocked violently. The smell of rotten eggs and gas filled my nose as the back of the boat belched flames that turned the seawater to steam. We rocketed forward, eating the distance between the Twin Otter and us as it rose into the sky.

The indicator on the grappling hook went green a split second later, and I depressed the trigger. The big, boxy looking projectile burst from the front of the weapon, trailing a reed thin cord. It smacked into the flotilla at the bottom of the plane, an eye-blink before the last of the cable left the reel.

I was jerked off my feet and into the water. I skidded along the surface, struggling to hang on as waves pounded against me. My arm screamed in pain as the straps on my wrist that held the grappling gun in place bit into my skin.

Indescribable pain exploded through my arm as the plane left the ocean and sailed upward, hauling me into the air. I whipped around beneath the plane, realizing how close I'd been to being ripped to shreds by the ocean.

As the plane climbed up into the wild blue yonder, and I whipped around like a fishing line in the wind, I reached up with my free hand and hit the button on the side of the device. The line snapped taut, jerking me forward toward the plane.

A moment later, I slammed into the Twin Otter's skin hard enough to rattle my teeth. My vision went a touch blurry as I struggled to grab onto the flotilla with my other hand, but my fingers just scrabbled against the steel shell. I shut my eyes, trying to bite down the pain. Then I swung as hard as I could while reaching up. My fingers closed around one of the flotilla's brace-bars. I grabbed hold of it and managed to pull myself up onto the landing gear. I wrapped my body around it as I loosened the grappling cable enough to give me some space.

"Okay, Billy. Now that you're up here, how the

hell are you going to get inside?" I muttered through gritted teeth as the wind whipped by me.

The Twin Otter's main door was barely a foot away, but I wasn't sure how I could get it open. Worse, I had no idea how long the grappling cable would hold me in place, and if it broke, I'd fall a thousand feet into the ocean.

"Screw it," I said, pulling out the M16 I'd gotten from Max and pointing it at the door.

Only, before I could fire the door opened. A soldier stood there, a strange look on his face as he peered down at me. He had a giant magnum in one hand, but so far he wasn't pointing it at me.

"What are you doing here?" he asked, dumbfounded.

Instead of replying, I fired. The bullets punctured his chest, causing him to lose his balance and topple past me toward the ocean.

I released my hold on the gun, letting it catch on the strap around my shoulder and grabbed onto the bottom of the plane. I hauled myself into the vehicle as another soldier moved forward, gun at the ready. Only like his partner, he wasn't firing. Hell, he didn't even have a gun. I wasn't sure if it was because they were afraid of firing around the plane, but either way, his knife would be more than enough to take me down.

His machete glinted in the fluorescent light of the plane as I threw myself at him. I hit him around the waist like a bag of wet cement, and we slid across the small plane before smacking into the other side with enough force to leave me dazed and confused.

Things inside the cabin whipped around, getting sucked outside the door as the Twin Otter started to slow. A fist caught me square in the jaw while I was looking at the open door, and I toppled backward toward it. My hands lashed out, catching hold of a handhold on the ceiling and stopping me from tumbling outside as the soldier slashed at me with his machete.

I twisted away, but my arm got hung up on my own grappling cable, causing me to jerk back toward the weapon. The blade caught me hard where the apparatus was attached to my arm, and my shoulder ached from the jolt of it.

As I toppled forward to the ground, it started to go nuts inside the section of the cabin we occupied as the pilot tried to compensate for the added friction of the open door.

The soldier whirled on me, bringing his knife up

as I threw myself back toward the door. Sailing through the opening, I pulled my M16 and unloaded it into his chest, sending him sprawling against the far wall. The cable around my wrist tightened, jerking me to a stop, and I plummeted toward the landing gear.

My chest crashed into it with enough force for my vision to go hazy. Breath rushed from my lungs as I hung there over the flotilla trying to remember how to breathe. After an inordinate amount of time, I somehow managed to pull myself back onto the landing gear and hoist myself back into the cabin once more.

Wind whipped around me as I threw one arm through a handhold and used my elbow to hold me in place while I removed the grappling hook's mounts. The sudden strain on my left hand was nearly enough to rip my arm off my entire body, but there was no way around it. I gritted my teeth and reached out for the door with my right hand. The moment my fingers touched the door, I grabbed the handle and hauled on it with everything I had.

Some kind of door assist kicked in, and the door slid shut, sealing me inside the cabin. I collapsed to my knees huffing as the plane righted itself.

The sound of the two guards rushing toward the door sealing off this section of the plane was barely audible over the wind whipping around outside the cabin, and part of me was glad they hadn't started shooting. Then again, maybe they didn't know what had happened to their friends.

I crouched down as best I could beside the door, trying to find a vantage point that wouldn't have me getting shot the second the door opened. Then I waited.

As the door inside the cabin opened, I fired my M16 until it clicked empty. The hail of bullets caught the first guard in the chest, knocking him off his feet. He crashed into his partner, throwing him off balance too. I stood and raced forward, dropping the M16 onto its strap as I pulled my Glock 19. Two shots put the stumbling partner down as I moved toward to the door in a low crouch.

As I passed through, I saw a girl dressed in sheer, practically see-through garment like some kind of slutty Princess Jasmine from Aladdin. She was beautiful in that whole Arabian princess way with long black hair and dark, mysterious eyes.

"Stop," she said, stepping between me and the door on the far side of the plane and raising one slender hand. "If you move one more step, I, Aliya

Masih, chief assassin to Abbad Tahan, will kill you."

"I'm looking for Annabeth. Where is she?" I asked, pointing my Beretta at her pretty face. I didn't care how deadly she was, I'd kill her in a heartbeat to save Ren's daughter.

"It doesn't matter where she is. This is where your heroism dies, American," she said, her words breathless and angry. "This is my command, and so it will be."

"What do you mean it's your command?" I replied. "What are you talking about?"

"This plane belongs to my employer, and he has purchased this cargo through the proper channels." She shook her head. "You are interfering with the proper ways now. For that, you will die."

"You're forgetting one thing," I said as she took another step toward me.

"What's that?" she asked, quirking a perfect eyebrow at me.

I pulled the trigger on my Glock, blowing her pretty face into a million blood-soaked fragments. "I'm the one with the gun."

As I stepped over her body and opened the door to the next room, I gasped. The room was straight out of an Arabian harem movie. It was filled with lush red silk pillows with all to wall couches. Only, instead of scantily-clad women lounging upon them, two more women dressed like the one I'd shot were busy wrangling a redheaded college girl into a costume like theirs. Bits and pieces of clothing were everywhere.

"Where's Annabeth?" I asked, raising my Glock, pointing it at the left assassin girl, and pulling the trigger. The bullet caught her between the shoulder-blades, pitching her forward onto the shirtless redhead she was grappling with.

As the report of the gunshot rang out, the other one let go of the girl and turned to regard me with cold, angry eyes.

"Who is Annabeth?" she snarled, eyes flicking from me to the dead girl and back again.

"She's with Abbad," the redhead cried, and as she raised her hand to point toward the door at the far end of the room, the wannabe Princess Jasmine slapped her across the face.

I pulled the trigger without a second thought, sending the lady into the afterlife. As she crumbled to the ground, I moved toward the door.

"Thank you!" the redhead cried. Her eyes were huge and tear-filled. "We thought we were dead."

"Is Annabeth through there?" I asked, pointing

at the door. I hadn't even known the plane was this compartmentalized, but this one had to be some kind of custom job.

"Yes," she nodded to me. "She told him she'd go with him if they left me alone, but once he took her in there…" She glared at the broken bodies of the two assassins. "They lied…" She swallowed. "I'm Samantha by the way."

"Here, Samantha," I said, reaching into my holster and pulling out my second Glock. I offered it to her. "Use this if something goes wrong."

As Samantha took the gun from me, I moved toward the door. While part of me wanted to stay here and help the girl, Annabeth still needed me.

"Okay," she said, moving toward the back of the cabin with her gun. From the way she held it, I was betting she'd never so much as fired one before. Hopefully, that wouldn't change. "Good luck."

"Thanks." I grabbed hold of the door and pulled it open to find myself looking at a chamber similar to the one I'd just been in.

A huge Middle Eastern looking man wearing a custom black suit stood toward the back with one arm around Annabeth's neck. Her face was twisted in fear and tears streamed down her cheeks while a self-satisfied smile filled his goateed face. The son of a bitch was using her as a human shield.

"If you do anything, I will kill her." He had one of those smug, "my money makes me better than regular folk" voices. "I'm not joking." He pressed the tip of a knife into Annabeth's ribs.

Similar to the girls I'd shot, Annabeth was dressed in a pair of see-through pink pants and a matching top that left little to the imagination. I fought the urge to look away out of common decency, but I didn't want to give the bastard a chance to do something to me.

Fury washed over me, distilling everything down to his stupid, conceited face. I was going to tear his goddamned head off.

"How can you do this to these women?" I snarled, barely able to recognize my own voice.

"I can do whatever I want to them. I have paid for them. They are mine." He pressed the point of the blade into Annabeth's side, drawing a gasp from her. His dark eyes flashed with amusement.

"No one gets to own another person!" I snarled, pointing my Glock at him.

"You can think whatever you want, but they are mine to do with as I wish." He shrugged and gestured insolently at me with his knife. "That is the way of the world. Money trumps all things."

As I narrowed my eyes at him, Annabeth elbowed him in the gut and squirmed away. I fired at him as he dropped to the ground. The bullet shattered the window in the safety door behind him.

Wind whipped around us, turning the inside of the plane into a wind tunnel. The Twin Otter listed sharply, causing me to lose my balance and careen toward Abbad. My Glock went flying from my hand as I slid across the plane and crashed into the cushioned wall.

That's when the door broke loose, tearing off the plane and spinning out into the blue sky. I tried to get my bearings, but my vision was a little too blurry and the floor a little too unsteady. Not that it mattered. Even if the pilots could land a plane with a hole in it, there was no way I was letting Abbad off this plane alive. Not after what he'd done to Ren's daughter. I just needed a way to make sure she and the other girl were safe first.

"Billy. Tell my dad I love him, okay?" Annabeth called from across the plane. She was on her hands and knees near Abbad who was already leveling a gun at me. He had his other hand wrapped around a seatbelt attached to the couch.

Before he could shoot me, Annabeth threw herself into Abbad as he fired. The bullet flew by my head, burying itself in the wall behind me as the two of them tumbled through the open door of the plane.

21

"No!" I screamed, and even though it was the stupidest thing I'd ever done, I rushed toward the open door of the plane.

As I moved, Samantha grabbed my arm, stopping me before I could be swept out of the plane.

"Please, you need to stay and help me," she said as I threw off her grip and grabbed the parachute off the wall next to the door.

I shoved my cellphone into her hand. "Call Max. He'll help you. Use the gun I gave you to make them land."

"You can't just leave me," she cried, dropping to her knees on the floor of the plane.

"Call Max," I said as I slung on the parachute. "He *will* help you."

I leapt out the door and careened down through the air, thankful the wind didn't tear me out of the hastily tightened straps. I snapped the buckles into place, tightening them as best as I could before lining my body up like a torpedo and heading straight for Annabeth and Abbad as they fell. They weren't much farther down than me, only about thirty meters or so, but it looked like a nearly insurmountable void.

As I torpedoed downward toward them, I tried to figure out how high up we were. If I had to guess, we were somewhere around four thousand feet in the air, well above the twenty-five-hundred-foot dives I'd done in training.

Even still, given the water below, I could save her as long as I reached her before we hit about a thousand feet, maybe more if this rig was designed to deploy quickly. Hell, I hadn't even had time to check to see how the chute was packed. Would it even open?

Only I couldn't worry about that now. I had to get to her.

When Abbad saw me, he grabbed onto Annabeth and pulled her to him. As his arms and legs wrapped around her, I realized the bastard just wanted to take her with him.

Worse, while I couldn't even shoot him for fear of hitting Annabeth, he didn't have that problem. His gun came up, and he fired. The bullet shot by me, and I elongated my body, trying to speed toward him as we fell through the sky a few thousand feet above the ocean. Another bullet whistled by me, and I gritted my teeth.

I was only a few meters away now. As Abbad lined up his next shot, Annabeth elbowed the smug bastard in the jaw. His head snapped to the side, and he lost his grip on Annabeth, giving me enough space to risk a shot. My round caught him in the side of the head, blowing his brains out over the ocean.

Their two bodies drifted apart, and I redoubled my effort to catch her. We were closing in on what seemed like two thousand feet at an alarming rate. There wasn't much time left. I had to get to her now! The sea rushed toward me as Annabeth reached out with one hand.

"I've got you!" I cried, stretching my hand toward hers. My fingers brushed against the tips of hers.

"Billy!" she screamed as I grabbed onto her wrist.

Her other hand came up and seized my wrist as

I pulled her up against my body and wrapped my legs around her waist.

"Hang on!" I cried and jerked on the parachute release cord. It didn't open. Instead, the cord came free in my hand. My breath caught in my throat as the ocean below surged up toward us, and I watched in horror as we got closer to what I judged was the fifteen-hundred-foot mark.

"Billy, do something!" Annabeth cried as I pulled on the emergency cord.

The parachute opened, catching the wind and hauling us upward. Annabeth slipped, but I grabbed onto her, holding on with everything I had.

"Hang on!" I told her as the wind buffeted against us.

"I am!" she said as I wrapped myself around her, bracing for impact as we crashed into the ocean.

22

Our impact with the Caribbean Sea smashed the air from my lungs and beat my body to hell and back again. It hurt so much, I could barely think past the pain. As we plunged into the water, Annabeth slipped away, and as I reached for her, the surf wind caught hold of my parachute and twisted it around me.

I shook myself into action, thankful the parachute had slowed our descent enough to keep me from breaking anything or getting knocked unconscious. My hand went to my waist, and I hit the button on the Zephyr Self-Inflating Personal Flotation Device. The CO_2 canister fired at once, filling it with upwards of fifteen pounds of flotation.

"Put that on and inflate it," I said, grabbing the spare Zephyr and tossing it to Annabeth who was dog paddling a few meters away. It landed with a splash a few feet from her.

"Okay!" she called back and started swimming toward the inflatable life preserver.

As my hands went to the snaps of the parachute harness, the wind caught hold of the parachute and dragged me backward. Waves pounded me, making it nearly impossible to release myself thanks to the force of the straps against my body. Water hit me in the face as I whipped around, making it nearly impossible to catch my breath. If I hadn't had the Zephyr I'd just be dead.

I snatched my knife, a SOG Aegis Mini, from the sheath and flipped it open. Twisting as best I could while the parachute dragged me across the ocean, I slashed at the parachute's mainline with the serrated edge. The ocean jolted me again as the wind died down enough for me to sever the line and free myself. Annabeth was in the distance, paddling toward me.

As I started swimming back toward her, a dorsal fin jutted from the ocean just behind her.

"Shark!" I screamed, flailing at her as the massive creature angled toward her.

Annabeth froze as the shark surged toward her, maw agape to reveal its razor-sharp teeth. I pulled my spare Glock from its holster and fired at it. The gunshot rang out as the water near the shark exploded into a spray of salty water, causing it to veer off course.

I kicked hard, moving toward Annabeth as quickly as I could while the shark angled around for another try. Annabeth swam as hard as she could, but I knew it wouldn't matter because neither of us were faster than the oceanic predator.

It came surging forward, its massive twenty-foot gray body cutting through the ocean like a hot knife through butter. I fired again, unloading three more shots into the ocean. Even though my bullets had an effective range of about three feet once they hit the water, the shark changed course to avoid her once again. Only this time, instead of heading off into the distance, it came toward me.

"Shoot it!" Annabeth cried as she swung around to watch the shark while I hoped beyond all hope it would just go away.

"I'm trying," I cried, emptying the pistol to no avail into the water as the monster barreled forward, all teeth and fury.

Its cold, flat eyes glinted menacingly in the glare of the sun as it moved to take a bite out of me. I threw my body to the side at the last second, narrowly avoiding its hideous, gaping maw and jammed my SOG into the creature's gills. The knife tore through the shark's flesh as it surged past me, spilling crimson into the water. It snapped, gnashing its teeth as the knife was ripped from my hand.

"Swim! Now!" I yelled, kicking toward Annabeth. She watched me for a split second before swimming with much more natural grace than I could manage, even though she was also wearing a fully-inflated Zephyr.

"Billy," she called, voice labored and fearful. "What if it comes back?"

"Then I'll splash around like a wounded animal to draw it to me," I said as I finally reached her.

"Do you think it's gone?" she asked, gazing past me toward the ocean. I turned my head back toward where the shark should have been, but I couldn't see it anymore. I wasn't sure if that was a good thing or a bad thing.

"Maybe… but either way, I really hope it was alone," I murmured, mostly to myself as I lay back and let the Zephyr hold me up. There was nowhere to swim to, and if Max couldn't find me based on the tracker I had, it wouldn't matter, anyway.

"If there are others, maybe they'll decide the one you stabbed is prey," Annabeth said hopefully before pulling me forward. "Come on, let's at least try to put some distance between us and the blood. I know they can smell it for miles, but still…"

"I supposed you're right." That thought chilled me to the core. I forced myself to be calm even though I was sure I smelled like blood.

One breath in. One breath out.

We began to swim.

23

"I think it might be time for us to consider the fact that there may be no rescue," I said as we lay in the water. I had Annabeth's hand clasped in mine as we stared up at the sky. So far, no more sharks had come along, which was good. While I might be able to deal with one, there was no way I'd be able to fight off an entire feeding frenzy.

"It's only been a couple hours. Maybe your friend will still find us," Annabeth said, looking at me and smiling. "And even if they don't, I'm glad anyway." She shivered. "I do not want to think about what would have happened if you hadn't shown up when you did."

"I'm sorry it wasn't sooner," I said, turning to look at her.

"Billy, if there's one thing I know about you, it's that you don't wait." She smiled at me, and it was like the Florida sunrise. "I *know* you did everything you could."

"I should have done more," I said, and as she opened her mouth to reply, I held up my free hand. "I mean that. I need you to know how sorry I am…" I swallowed. "About this…"

"Billy, you can't keep apologizing for that." She shook her head. "These might be our last moments together, and I don't want to spend them hashing out what we should have both done differently because Lord knows I'm no saint either." She took a deep breath and squeezed my hand. "Though, I will admit, I'd hoped I'd kick the bucket a few years from now."

"I suppose you're right," I said as the sound of a boat filled my ears. Relief shot through me at the sound, and while part of me worried it might be the bad guys, I almost didn't care. Bad guys I could fight. An ocean? Not so much.

We both turned as the Princess Pearl pulled up beside us, and my heart leapt for joy. Max stood on the edge of the boat, and I could see Samantha on the deck.

"Sorry it took you so long," Max called, tossing

a life-ring toward me. He jerked a thumb back at Samantha. "Had to get her from the plane once it landed."

"I'm just glad you came," I said, taking a deep breath. "I mean that. We'd be dead otherwise."

"You'd have done the same for me, Billy," Max said, nodding to me. "But I'll gladly let you buy me a pint."

"Consider it done," I said. "That's the best deal this side of the equator."

I hooked one arm through the ring while wrapping my other around Annabeth. Max hit a button on the side of his boat, starting the winch attached to the life-ring. Annabeth gripped me with both hands, threading her arms around my body to keep us together. The cord began to retract, pulling us toward the ladder Max had dropped over the side of the boat.

We reached it a moment later, and I hung back, treading water while Annabeth made her way up the ladder. As Max pulled her on board, I grabbed hold of the rungs and began climbing. It was harder than I expected since I was tired, soaking wet, and still laden with a bunch of gear, but I managed it anyway.

By the time I pulled myself over the railing and

into the boat itself, my chest was heaving for breath. I flopped down onto one of the benches as Mary Ann appeared from the cockpit. She wrapped a giant white towel around Annabeth who was sitting on the far bench next to Samantha.

As Max offered Annabeth a bottle of water, she took it and opened the cap before looking at me. "Billy, you drink some first." She held the bottle out.

"There's no way in Hell, I'm doing that," I said, shaking my head at her. "You drink, okay?" I gestured toward Max as he rummaged around in his ice chest. "I'm fairly certain he's got more, anyway."

"Okay." She nodded and took a sip, then another, and before I knew it, she'd drained the entire half-liter.

"Thirsty?" Max asked, holding another bottle out to me. Condensation glistened along the plastic, and I took it from him.

"Yes," I said, taking the bottle as Mary Ann flopped down on the bench next to me with another towel.

Max turned to Annabeth. "I can get you another, if you like?"

"You should get her another one anyway,"

Mary Ann said before turning to smile at me. "You did it, Billy."

"Now, what's a fine girl like you doing on a boat like this?" I asked, pulling her close.

"I can drive if the two of you need some time," Max said, putting a hand on my shoulder as he moved past us toward the cockpit. "Probably better that way anyway."

Mary Ann pulled back then, and shot him a look. "You have no idea how to handle a vessel like this, Max. Get out of the way before you hurt yourself." She shot me one last fleeting look before getting to her feet.

"I'm not one to argue with a lady," Max said, stepping aside to let Mary Ann into the cockpit.

"Say, how'd you get her down so quickly?" I asked, glancing from Max to Samantha as she sat huddled next to Annabeth on the other bench. The two of them were talking in whispers I couldn't hear, but at my words, Samantha looked over at me.

"I called him like you said, Billy," Samantha said. Her cheeks were awash with color, making the freckles on her nose stand out. "He told me to hand the phone to the pilot. I did, and the next thing I knew, we'd landed back at the dock." She bit her lip and looked away then.

I turned my eyes to Max and raised an eyebrow. He gave me one nod. "I wanted to talk to you about that, actually."

"What do you mean?" I asked, finishing my water and wiping my mouth with the back of one hand. "Is there a problem?"

"Yes and no." Max moved to sit down next to me as Mary Ann started the Princess Pearl and began motoring off. "The problem is this place. We can't exactly hand them over without a lot of awkward questions that will lead the Jamaican government right to you." He sighed. "So, I don't know what to do, especially since I'm betting some very not nice people will want to talk to them."

"Are you saying what I think you're saying?" I asked as Max reached out and put his hand on my shoulder.

"I think we should take the lot of them somewhere safe and set them up with witness protection. I think that's what Ren would want. I tried to ask him, but I haven't gotten ahold of him yet." He met my eyes, and I could see the thoughts swimming through them. "I have a buddy who can help with that."

"I think it's a good idea," Mary Ann said, and I

looked past Max to see her looking back at us from behind the wheel of the Princess Pearl.

"You do?" I asked, regarding her thoughtfully. "It will upend everyone's lives…"

I shut my eyes for a second, letting my thoughts rattle around in my brain. Part of me knew Max was right, that the girls' safety was the most important thing. Only, I didn't feel right about it without Ren around.

"I don't know if Ren will want Annabeth to go," I said, opening my eyes and swallowing hard. "And what about her parents?" I turned my eyes to Max as I gestured at Samantha.

"You make a fair point, but I'm overriding you, Billy," he said, shaking his head at me. "Let me get them somewhere safe for a while. Once you get ahold of Ren, we can talk. Until then, they'll be safe and sound. I'll make sure of it, Billy. You have my word." He met my eyes. "You know what that's worth."

"Okay," I said, getting to my feet and crossing the distance to him and holding out my hand. "I don't like this, but I trust you, Max. If you think it's for the best, do it."

"Good," Max said, moving into the cockpit and putting his hand on the wheel. "Mary Ann, spend some time with Billy. I think I can manage this until we get to my friend."

Mary Ann looked at him for a long time before nodding. "When will we get to your friend?"

"A couple hours?" Max shrugged. "I already called him. He's on his way to Jamaica. I'm sure everything will be arranged by the time he arrives on the island."

"Okay," she said, nodding at him before turning back to me. She came over and sat down next to me, putting her head against my shoulder and snuggling against me. Her warmth filled me with a strange sort of desperation. "Billy, will you hold me until we get there?"

"Even if the whole world tries to tear me from your side," I replied, swallowing as she looked up at me.

"Good," she said, reaching around my waist and pulling me close to her body. She looked up into my eyes while biting her lip. Mary Ann touched my face gently with her free hand, drawing me down to her, while her other hand traced along my back. She kissed me.

Unlike before, this wasn't hungry or desperate. It was all things to all people. It was a bird's first flight from the nest, a sunrise over mountain tops.

Sign up to my newsletter here. If you do, I'll let you know when the next book comes out.

Visit me on Facebook or on the web at JohnnyAsa.com for all the latest updates.

74047689R00144

Made in the USA
Middletown, DE
19 May 2018